ROSA FIELDI

Rosa enjoyed the ride in
and so affectionate that she consid
ate girl. He wanted to know how Mrs Trabb had executed
his orders with regard to her wardrobe and, in his anxiety to
know if everything was nice and proper, actually commenced to investigate Rosa's underclothing.

'And now, Rosa darling,' said the ancient voluptuary, 'let
me see if Mrs Trabb has obeyed my orders about your
trousers, I told her to have them made a certain way or you
were to wear none at all.'

'Oh, dear me, Mr Bonham,' exclaimed Rosa, who all this
time had been dutifully holding up her clothes to facilitate
her guardian's exploration, 'you will make me ashamed of
myself!'

ROSA FIELDING: VICTIM OF LUST

Anonymous

A STAR BOOK

published by
the Paperback Division of
W.H. ALLEN & Co PLC

A Star Book
Published in 1984
by the Paperback Division of
W.H. Allen & Co. PLC
44 Hill Street, London W1X 8LB

Typeset by Phoenix Photosetting, Chatham
Printed and bound in Great Britain by
Cox & Wyman Ltd, Reading

ISBN 0 352 31544 X

This book is sold subject to the condition that it shall not,
by way of trade or otherwise, be lent, re-sold, hired out or
otherwise circulated without the publisher's prior consent in
any form of binding or cover other than that in which it is
published and without a similar condition including this condition
being imposed upon the subsequent purchaser.

Chapter I

It was a fine morning in May, and the dull, little frequented High Street of the small country town called Rutshole seemed absolutely cheerful, as if inspired by the exhilarating atmosphere.

So at least thought Mr Bonham, a portly widower of fifty or thereabouts, as having left his carriage at the inn, he proceeded down High Street leisurely, but with the usual solemnity on his countenance, (which he considered dignified and respectable) much lightened by the cheering weather. He stopped at the door of a small shop, on which was inscribed, 'Trabb, Hosier and Glover'. Here he entered.

Now that capital woman of business, the widow Trabb, was engaged in suiting a stiff-necked old maid with a pair of mittens; but even if she had not been so occupied, we very much doubt if she would herself have attended to a gentleman customer. The worthy woman knew that there are other means of making a shop attractive besides the excellence and cheapness of the wares therein sold: and she had enlisted in her services a pretty girl of sixteen, whose remarkable grace and modesty had already attracted numerous young squires, young farmers, and officers from the neighbouring garrison town, as real or pretended customers, to the manifest advantage of Mrs Trabb's till.

When therefore, she saw the rich and respectable Mr Bonham enter her shop, she summoned her aide-de-camp with 'Rosa, attend to the gentleman!' and continued her attention to her customer. Now Mr Bonham, though nearly fifty as we have said, and of a very staid and even strict outward demeanour, was by no means so elderly in his feelings and capabilities as would have been judged from outward appearances. He had been early left a widower, and the very fact of his having to keep up the said outward appearances and his ambition to have a saintly character among his neighbours and friends, had forced him to restrain his indulgences within very narrow bounds, and to be circumspect and moderate in the enjoyment thereof. So that this self denial was of a double benefit to him; among the saints of his acquaintance he was esteemed as 'one of the elect and a babe of grace', while he himself was pleasingly conscious that, thanks to his regular but very generous diet, and his habit of self control (not abstinence) as to the softer sex, he was enjoying what is called a green old age; and was when on the verge of fifty, pretty confident that his latent powers when called into action would be found quite equal to those of many a worn out young roué of five and twenty.

He was remarkably struck with Rosa's beauty, and well he might be. Long, flowing, golden hair; deep blue eyes, a sweet but by no means insipid expression of face, combined with a graceful figure, and manners very attractive even in her humble occupation; all detained Mr Bonham in purchasing a pair of gloves, longer than he had ever been in his life before. Certainly he was very difficult to suit; and Rosa had to take the measurements of his hand more than once. At last he was suited – as far as gloves were concerned – and was about to leave the shop when a bright idea struck him. He turned back to where Mrs Trabb was standing, that estimable woman had just got rid of her Low Church looking customer triumphantly, she had clapped two pence extra onto the price of the mits, and then after some bargaining submitted to rebate a penny. So both parties were satisfied, and Mrs T felt not only 'at peace with all men' (that she generally was) but with all women too (which was not so frequently the case).

'Mrs Trabb,' began the respectable gentleman, 'I would like to consult you about a little matter of business that may be a source of gain to a trades woman in your line; besides being conducive to the moral benefit of a tribe of benighted heathens.'

'Dear me, Mr Bonham,' exclaimed the gratified hosier, 'step this way – very kind of you I'm sure – a glass of cherry brandy? – do now – and sit down and rest yourself.'

So saying, she ushered the artful old gentleman into her snug back parlour; and producing the refreshment alluded to, awaited further disclosures.

We will not weary the reader with a full account of the proposed mercantile transaction. Suffice it to say that Mr Bonham disclosed a case of soulharrowing destitution among the Fukkumite Islanders recently converted to Christianity.

The interesting females had not the wherewithal to cover their bare bottoms, but used to display those well rounded features to the unhallowed gaze of the unregenerate sailors of whale ships calling at the islands. Now the missionaries considered that if any bottoms were to be displayed by their precious converts, the exhibition should be made in private to their spiritual advisers. And to end the story, the benevolent gentleman, by way of advancing the moral and physical comforts of the Fukkumite ladies (to say nothing of the missionaries) asked Mrs Trabb if she would like to contract for the supply of say to begin with, one thousand pairs of frilled pantalettes.

'Really very kind of you, Mr Bonham, to give me such a chance,' said the gratified shopkeeper, 'but may I ask you, sir, if the creatures, or converts, or whatever is most proper to call them, are to wear nothing else but those trousers?'

'No, I believe not,' was the answer. 'Why?'

'Because sir,' replied the experienced widow, 'a woman's pants are made, to speak plainly, with openings at the front and rear, corresponding to her natural openings; so really, though I shall be very glad to undertake the contract, I must tell you before hand, for fear of having my goods thrown back on my hands, that the garments proposed are no obstruction whatever to a man who is determined to violate a woman.'

'Very proper of you to make the remark, Mrs Trabb, very business-like and fair; but then of course the women should have opportunities for performing their natural functions conveniently; and then our self-sacrificing brethren, the missionaries, they must have facilities for their comforts.'

'Oh, of course, Sir,' was the response.

'Then send in your estimate, Mrs Trabb, I'll see that you have a good chance. By the bye, Mrs Trabb, who is that modest looking and rather attractive young person who attended to my requirements in your shop just now?'

Aha! thought the sharp widow, that's it, eh? (Rather caught I should think.)

'That young woman, sir, is a daughter of the Fieldings. You know, sir, farmers about three miles from here. Rosa her name is – a very nice girl and as good as she looks. Take another glass, sir!'

4

'No, thank you, Mrs Trabb, send in those estimates as soon as you can and good luck to you.'

Exit Bonham.

The very next morning he mounted his fine weight-carrying cob and riding out leisurely, as if for exercise, had no sooner got out of sight and hearing of Rutsden Lodge, as his residence was termed, and out of the ken of his sharp daughter Eliza, than he spurred his good hackney into a smart trot, which pace being occasionally varied by a canter, very soon brought him to Elm-Tree Farm.

Farmer Fielding was out, which his visitor was not altogether very sorry for, as he thought it would be better in every way to begin his tactics by talking the old lady over. She received him very kindly and hospitably, though evidently puzzled to know the object of his visit. Mr Bonham was not long in breaking ground, for he knew the farmer might return in five minutes. He recounted to the gratified mother how he had been struck by the elegant yet modest and quiet appearance of Rosa, and how he was pleased to learn from Mrs Trabb, that she was as good as she looked; that notwithstanding the great respectability of Mrs T and her establishment, and the high opinion he had of her moral worth, still he could not but be aware that a position behind her counter was pernicious, if not absolutely dangerous, to a girl of Rosa's attractive personal qualities.

'Why my dear Madam,' urged the moralist, 'I am informed that the young squires and farmers will ride a couple miles out of their way to deal in Mrs Trabb's shop; and then those dragoon officers come all the way from Baboonfield Barracks. I know that man of Moab, their Colonel, Earl Phuckum the first, gets all his clothes from London, and I'd like to know what he wants in Mrs Trabb's in High Street.'

'Perhaps dear Rosy will make a good marriage,' simpered the fond and foolish mother.

'Perhaps, madam,' interposed Mr Bonham sternly, 'she may learn something what ought to come after marriage but never before. How would you like to hear of her bolting off to London with one of those swells who perhaps is married already, and her returning to you in about twelve months, neglected, sick and heartbroken, with a baby in her arms? Now listen to me, Mrs Fielding,' continued Mr Bonham, gazing attentively into the good dame's horror-stricken face, 'I am not too old to have my fancies. Moreover, my daughter will soon be married and off my hands, and I have no one else to interfere with me.'

With this introduction, the model gentleman proposed a scheme of his own, namely that Rosa should be placed in a first-rate school in the neighbourhood of London; that all the expenses, including her equipment, should be borne by him; and that in twelve or eighteen months, if Rosa had been well behaved and steady, and had improved in body and mind, as there was every reason to suppose she would, he, the speaker, would make her Mrs Bonham, and mistress of Rutsden Lodge.

This grand proposition fairly took away the good old lady's breath, and there is no doubt her reply would have been a ready acceptance of Mr Bonham's proposition but then there appeared old Fielding and the whole story had to be commenced over again.

He did not receive Mr Bonham's offer as enthusiastically as his wife had done; but he owned at the same time the risk that Rosa ran in her present situation; and in plain blunt speech detailed how Susan Shufflebum had been seen behind a hayrick with her legs over young Squire Rootlepole's back.

'And I suppose, missus,' continued the worthy man,

'I needn't tell ye what he was a-doing to her; and Harriette Heavely went a-walking in Snugcroft woods with one of the danged soger officers, and when she got home her white petticoats was all green with damp grass, and she was so sore between her thighs that she has not been able to walk rightly since. But still, Master Bonham, although your proposal would take our Rosa out of the way of danger; leastways out of a good deal, for a young good-looking lass is never to say quite out of danger; yet I don't quite like the girl brought up above her station. She'll maybe look down on her old father and mother, and maybe she'll be looked down upon and made to feel the difference by them that's born of better families.'

This sensible speech of Farmer Fielding's was combated pretty sharply by the other two parties to the conversation; the old woman being anxious to see her daughter made a rich lady, and loth to miss the present chance; and Mr Bonham continuing to urge that his being almost entirely without relations and that his daughter being about to be married, would place Rosa in a far different and much more pleasant situation than is usually the case under such circumstances. He even went on to say that although Fielding had a right to deal as he liked with regards to his own daughter, yet he considered it would be almost sinful for him to throw away such a good chance to have her well educated and married, and that too in the fear of the Lord. Half badgered to death between the pair of them – the old farmer yielded a reluctant consent, upon which Mr Bonham and Mrs Fielding went at once into matters of detail with regard to preparation of outfit and so on.

One thing was determined upon, that the matter might not be talked about more than was absolutely necessary; Mr Bonham in particular to conceal his philanthropic schemes from his daughter Eliza, lest peradventure she had been addicted to wrath. And Farmer

Fielding thought that the less said about Rosa until she appeared as Mrs Bonham the better.

We do not intend to weary our readers as to matters of outfit, suffice it to say that Mrs Trabb was in high glee and began to think that Mr Bonham, what with his missionary zeal on behalf of the sweet Fukkumite savages, and his philanthropic intentions regarding Rosa's welfare was going to make her fortune. Certainly she never had had two such orders in one twelvemonth, much less in one week. One remark of hers to Mr Bonham is worthy of notice.

With the natural sharpness of a woman and a widow to boot, she took it for granted that Mr B would like to know some particulars about the under-garments she had been furnishing for his pretty protegee, and after expatiating for about an hour or so about silk stockings, cotton stockings, chemises, night-dresses, petticoats, and the Lord only knows what besides, she concluded with:

'And I quite remember your sensible remarks Mr Bonham, about those trousers made for those converted cannibals. Miss Rosa's are much finer of course, and prettier altogether, but they are equally convenient, they are quite open back and front.'

This remark was made with a good deal of emphasis and meaning; but the venerable Philanthropist merely replied, without moving a muscle of his face:

'You are quite right, Mrs Trabb, and have acted very judiciously; one never knows what may be required in case of emergency!'

It was reported to a few friends and neighbours that Rosa was offered a situation in London as a nursery governess and that as Mr Bonham was going to town on business he had kindly offered to convey the young lady thither in his own carriage; being, as he said, altogether safer and pleasanter for a young unprotected girl than the public conveyance. This excuse passed currently enough, and if some of the envious or captious neighbours shook their heads and said Old Bonham was a sly fox, what business was it of theirs, after all?

Rosa enjoyed the ride immensely. Her guardian, as she took to calling him, was so kind and so affectionate (the fact was that he kept kissing her a great many times, and much more warmly than there was any occasion for) that she considered herself a very fortunate girl. And then he took such an interest in minor matters, he wanted to know how Mrs Trabb had executed his orders – with regard to her wardrobe – and in his anxiety to know if everything was nice and proper, actually commenced to investigate Rosa's underclothing. He expressed his opinion that the petticoats would do; but that the outer one was hardly fine enough, but that defect could be repaired in London; his researches became more interesting when the chemise was put upon its trial.

'And now, Rosa darling,' said the ancient voluptuary, 'let me see if Mrs Trabb has obeyed my orders about your trousers, I told her to have them made a certain way or you were to wear none at all.'

'Oh, dear me, Mr Bonham,' exclaimed Rosa, who all this time had been dutifully holding up her clothes to facilitate her guardian's exploration, 'you will make me ashamed of myself!'

'Not at all, my dear girl,' was the reassuring reply, 'it is my duty to see that you have everything nice and proper, and your duty to submit to the enquiry; so put your graceful right leg over my left shoulder.'

Trembling and blushing, the innocent girl, fancying that it was not quite right and yet not knowing very well how to refuse, did as she was requested and made a splendid exposure of her secret parts immediately.

'Ha!' exclaimed Bonham, 'I see that Mrs Trabb has

not neglected her duty; your trousers are well open in front certainly, though for the sake of seeing your thighs I would have preferred no trousers at all. But your cunt shows very nicely – golden hair, I see – not quite as much as you will have in twelve months, but a very fair show for a young girl of sixteen, – and very nice lips.'

Here the moral gentleman inserted the first two fingers of his right hand in Rosa's tender orifice, at which the poor girl could not help an exclamation and making some slight appearance of resistance. On this her companion remarked:

'As you are going to be married to me in twelve or eighteen months, my lovely Rosa, I regard you already as my wife, morally speaking, and if the jolting of this carriage will allow, I will give you a practical proof of it.'

'A practical proof sir?' stammered Rosa.

'Yes, my beloved child, look here!' So saying, he unfastened his trousers and brought to view his cock, and a very good, useful, stiff-standing, domestic piece of machinery it was.

'Take hold of it, my little pet, do not be afraid, it won't hurt you.'

'What is it?' asked Rosa, who had never seen anything like it before, but who was clasping it as she was told, in a way that was increasing the weapon materially in size and stiffness.

'How hot it is,' she remarked.

'Yes love,' said her guardian, 'he is rather feverish, and there is considerable irritation, but you have a little warm bath between those lovely thighs of yours; and he will be quite cured after I have plunged him in and let him soak a couple of minutes.'

'I shall be very glad, my dear guardian, to do anything to contribute to your comfort or to show my gratitude for the kindness you have done me; but I do, I certainly do think that this thing, this part of your person, (I hardly know what to call it) is far too large to go into the slit between my thighs – which just now you called my cunt. Of course, you have a right to do as you please with me, and are perfectly welcome; but I fear you will hurt me dreadfully, even if you do not actually split my belly open, or extend my little orifice as far back as my bottom hole.'

'No fear, my sweet charmer,' replied her guide, philosopher and friend, 'your sweet orifice is destined by Providence for these assaults, and is wonderfully elastic; there is no risk therefore of my splitting your belly up or knocking your two holes into one – I should be very sorry to destroy such an elegant specimen of nature's handiwork, especially as I hope to live and to enjoy you for fifteen years to come – so open your thighs as wide as you can possibly stretch them, with your feet placed upon the opposite seat.'

Trembling, but obedient, the girl did as she was required, producing, as any of our readers will find, if they choose to try the experiment, a very favourable position.

(N.B. Should the seat on which the lady's bottom is situated be too high, a small carpet bag, a folded cloak, or an extra cushion under the gentleman's knees will raise him to the desired height.)

After this slight digression, let us proceed. However confidently Mr Bonham might have expressed himself as to his facilities of entrance into Rosa's virgin sanctuary he still did not neglect the only precautions which were at hand. It had never been his intention, until stimulated by the girl's outward graces and secret charms, to violate Rosa in his carriage, and therefore he had not provided himself with any cold cream or pomade, so the only lubricant he possessed was his mouth, and of that he proceeded to make such good use, that his pretty friend, who at first shrank nervously from the operation, as he proceeded, found it endurable, and at last actually began to like it, at least if her leaning complacently back with a half-smile upon her face, and endeavouring to stretch her thighs beyond their present extension could be interpreted as signs of such a feeling. We think so, and it is quite evident that her guardian thought so too, for murmuring to himself: 'Now's the time!' shifted his posture so as to bring his priapus and appendages into the situation just previously occupied by his mouth. The lips of Rosa's cunt were still open, and Mr Bonham had a fair chance and greatly to his credit he availed himself of it manfully. In he went about an inch and a half, and – there he stuck. Now had he attempted Rosa's maidenhood when first his prick came to full stand, we do not know what he might not have effected; but he had retained his member's tension too long, and had excited himself too much; consequently after getting in a short way as we have described, and making Rosa cry with his efforts against her barrier, his eager pushes were brought to a close in the most natural manner possible; viz. – by the arrival of the moment of delight, which certainly in this instance was a one-sided pleasure, and indeed hardly that, for we hold that even to give the man his proper share of transport, the injection must be performed when he is fairly within his companion, for spunking about the lips and mossy hair, or even an inch or so into the passage, as Mr Bonham did on this occasion, can hardly be called a satisfactory termination to a fuck. On this occasion it was not quite as bad as it might have been; for Rosa, who had gathered from some expressions of disappointment on the part of her friend, and a sort of intuitive feeling that all girls possess, that all was not right, was spared for the moment the pain of a burst maidenhood, and if her guardian was not quite satisfied, he was at least quieted, and that did quite as well, particularly as by this time the carriage was entering the suburbs of London – to say nothing of the risk of Thomas the coachman, or John the footman, becoming accidental spectators of his little game, and reporting him at home accordingly. So by his advice, Rosa wiped herself dry, and he looked as fatherly and demure as he could; and from his long practice in what we hardly choose to call hypocrisy but something very like it, succeeded very well. And by the time the carriage arrived at the gate of Mrs Moreen's Seminary for young ladies in Clapham nobody could have guessed from his manner that anything had transpired during the short journey irreconcileable with the fatherly manner he exhibited toward Rosa.

Mrs Moreen was most favourably impressed with his manner, and indeed was prepared to welcome him cordially, in consequence of the liberal arrangements entered into in the correspondence that had already passed between them.

She was also much interested in Rosa, being quite judge enough to see that, country bred and uneducated though she might be, she had all the capabilities of making a very elegant and showy young lady.

Leaving Rosa then thus happily situated; and her protector sitting down to a late dinner at a hotel in Covent Garden, for the old sinner made an excuse to himself for passing the night in London, being that his carriage horses would be knocked up by the return journey on the same day – besides, had he not business of some kind next morning? – leaving then these friends of ours so comfortable, we will return to Rutsden Lodge, and entering a small room where a tall, dashing-looking young lady with dark eyes and raven hair is writing a letter, we will take the privilege of narrators who are ex-officio invisible and ubiquitous, and

13

peep over a round white shoulder.

The letter began: 'My dearest Alfred,' and after a few ordinary remarks, got business-like and even warm.

'I am afraid,' the letter ran, 'that my father is going to make a fearful fool of himself. There was a baby-faced girl in a shop here and the old idiot, I fear, has seen her and fancied her. If he would only give her a fucking and a five pound note,' (this was the style the young lady wrote in,) 'there would be no harm done, but I believe, though don't know anything for certain – that she has got a governess's place in London, and he has conveyed her there in his carriage. He had to go up to town on business.

'Now I no more believe in his business than in her governess's situation – for she is not fit for one; and I believe the whole thing is a blind. And, what's more, her stupid old mother has been talking nonsense about her Rosa being a lady, all which, without being absolute proofs, make up a strong case against the old gentleman. Just fancy me with a mother-in-law! – a vulgar, uneducated country girl, about sixteen or seventeen years old. Of course, my dear Alfred, I know that you will marry me as soon as you can; indeed I think that in gratitude for the numerous privileges I have granted you, you should make a point of doing so – not that I regret that I allowed you to fuck me for I have enjoyed it very much, and trust entirely to your honour. But, then you see my dearest cousin, that somebody else can fuck besides you, and as sure as that stupid old party, my respected father, marries a young fresh country girl, he'll get her with child – just you see if he doesn't! And then my inheritance will be lessened at his death, or perhaps cut away altogether. And as for you, my dear cousin, you will come in simply for nothing at all. But you had better get a few days leave and come here on some pretext or other and we will have a consultation on

14

the subject. You see if you or some of your brother officers could get access to this girl, give her a good rogering
and get her with child, or turn her upon the town, it
would settle the question at once. And I think it might
be done. I will try to find out her address from that foolish old mother of hers. But do you come here at any
rate, my dearest Alfred; for I rather think that I want
something else besides a consultation; indeed the night
before last I had a dream about you, awoke with a wet
night-gown; so if you do come you had better take the
precaution of bringing a dozen preventatives in the
shape of French letters in your pocket. For I suppose
you will be wanting as usual to make the best use of your
privileges both as a cousin and an engaged lover; and I
know how those affectionate liberties usually termin-
ate.'

This was in effect the termination of the young lady's
letter, with the exception of a few strong and passionate
expressions of enduring attachment.

It was addressed to Captain Alfred Torrant, 51st
Dragoons, Baboonfield Barracks, where it was duly
received by that meritorious officer. He read it over
twice, so as to read, mark, learn and digest the contents;
then prudently and properly burnt it.

Then he relieved his feelings by swearing a good deal;
having by this precaution blown off any surplus steam,
he at once applied to his commanding officer for a few
days leave of absence, which was forthwith granted;
then he took his departure for Rutsden Lodge, travel-
ling in a dashing tandem, as a gentleman holding a com-
mission in HM's Dragoons ought to travel.

Chapter II

As the gallant Captain Torrant alighted from his dashing equipage, he was met at the hall door by Miss Bonham's attendant, a pretty, impudent girl, always ready to be kissed or pulled about by any handsome young gentleman, though habitually reserved and discreet with young men of her own station in life. She received the commander smiling, as he, as a matter of course gave her a kiss and a squeeze, together with his 'Good morning Lucy, how blooming you look today!'

'You had better keep all that sort of nonsense for my young lady, Captain Torrant!' was the reply, 'for I know she is expecting you!'

'How do you know that my dear?' enquired the dragoon.

'Easy enough,' replied the lady's maid, 'as I helped her to dress, she made me take out her prettiest morning frock, and moreover put on white stockings and her nice little bronze slippers. And I pretty well know what that means,' added the soubrette, archly nodding her head, as she tripped upstairs, leading the way to her young mistress's sitting room.

There the young captain was neither unexpected nor

unwelcome. We need not retire, as did the discreet Lucy after ushering in the guest, but remain witnesses to the affection, not to say transport, with which he was received by Miss Eliza Bonham.

'My own darling Alfred,' she exclaimed as she flung herself into his arms, kissing him most rapturously, 'how good of you to answer my note so quickly!'

Nor was the young gentleman one whit behind hand in reciprocating her profession of love. He glued his mouth to hers, pressed her to his breast, and even began with his right hand, which he purposely disengaged, to make a demonstration towards the lower part of her person. But this performance Eliza eluded, not from any dislike to the proceeding – oh, no! but from prudential motives.

'Stop, stop sir!' she laughingly exclaimed, 'not so fast, if you please – I understood you came here to talk over a disagreeable business matter; and besides, Alfred dear, you really must cover your beautiful instrument with that sheath, or condom, or whatever you call it. I have no notion of having a pretty white belly bow-windowed before marriage! – indeed I shan't particularly care about it after marriage!'

But the gallant young officer had not driven over from the barracks for nothing, and begged to assure his beautiful cousin that in his present state of mind and body, it would be quite impossible for him to give proper attention to any serious business, until his burning love for her received some temporary gratification, (the plain English of this being that he had a tremendous cock-stand, and felt that if it was not allayed pretty quickly that he must burst), and that as for the sheath, she might set her mind quite at rest, for he had brought a dozen with him.

'A dozen!' exclaimed Eliza, lifting up her eyes and hands in pretended astonishment, 'what on earth does the man mean by bringing a dozen? You are not going to fuck me a dozen times, I can tell you that, sir! And I don't want my waiting maid spoilt, mind that, and who else you intend to favour, of course I don't know—'

Here her speech was brought to an abrupt termination by her cousin covering her mouth with kisses and begging her to seat herself in a low easy chair, while he prepared himself for the promised treat. Fastening the door was a precaution taken as a matter of course, for Lucy knew that it was as much as her place was worth, to permit any intrusion in the neighbourhood, and Mr Bonham was not to arrive until the following day.

Coat off and trousers down, Alfred produced a bundle of safeguards, and selecting one of the filmy looking coverings, besought his lovely cousin to put it on for him. Of course he could have put it on himself perfectly well, but he was too great an epicure to miss any piquant delicacy in the approaching banquet. Accordingly, Eliza's delicate fingers as she performed the required office, added new fire to his already terribly inflamed prick, so that the scarlet knob absolutely turned purple and the whole nine inches, from the hardened balls to the orifice at the end, throbbed with excited lust. This was heightened by Eliza's appearance for, (being almost as eager as her gallant cousin, and that's saying a great deal), as she seated herself she drew up her clothes, and put one of her splendid legs over the chair on which she sat. Consequently, her rump being advanced quite to the extreme edge of the cushions, she made a most admirable display; her excitement and her lover's embraces had produced the usual result, and the lips of her cunt were slightly opened, temptingly inviting an entrance; while her bushy black hair showed off to advantage the creamy whiteness of her belly and thighs.

No wonder that as soon as the condom was securely

put on, Captain Torrant fell down on his knees, and expressed his adoration of the shrine he was going to enter by covering it with amorous kisses. Under this treatment, the pink lined portals expanded more and more and as Eliza flung back her head with a smile and a sigh, the young officer saw that the auspicious moment had arrived – not that he was an unwelcome visitor at any time in the mossy retreat, so getting his charger well in hand, he put his head straight for the gap and rushed in. It was indeed a short lived pleasure as may be conceived: the fact being that the gentleman was in that state of lust that two or three judicious rubs from the hand of his fair cousin would have released his evacuation; and as for the lady, if her hot lover had continued on his knees before her, kissing her cunt one half minute longer, he would have had some warm cream over his moustache, of a kind not generally sold by Rose or Gillingwater. So three good shoves, actually only three, did the business most effectually, and, no doubt to their great mutual satisfaction. But there was no mistake as to Miss Bonham's prudent regard to the sheath, or the Captain's good sense in acceding to her wishes.

For his beautiful antagonist met his attack so grandly and discharged her battery so promptly in reply to his, that if the latter had not been retained by the discreet covering, very serious consequences to the lady would have almost inevitably made themselves apparent in nine months' time or thereabouts.

And in our humble opinion gratification is not increased by running any risk. On the present occasion both Miss Bonham and her lover congratulated themselves on having enjoyed each other thoroughly, and without any fear of the result.

Their extreme transports being over for the present, the young gentleman applied himself to putting his dress in order, while Eliza rang the bell and desired Lucy to send up the lunch.

While this acceptable refreshment was being done justice to, the loving pair proceeded to consider what was to be done in regard to Mr Bonham's infatuation. Captain Torrant's first step was prompt and business like. He told his man Robert, a smart soldier, to take a walk through the fields in the neighbourhood of the Fielding's Farm, and, by getting into conversation with some of the farm lasses, he would most likely find out something as to Miss Rosa, the great probability being that the old dame would not be able to keep her mouth shut, but would have been dropping boastful hints as to her daughter's great prospects, being made a grand lady of, and so on.

'Find out this for me if you can Bob,' said his generous master, 'and I will give you free liberty to do what you like by way of amusing yourself with any of the girls.'

'Cert'nly sir, thank you sir,' replied that valuable domestic, saluting as he marched away on his errand.

Leaving him for a while to enjoy his country walk, we will attend at the consultation between the lovers.

'You see, my darling Alfred,' began Eliza, 'I fear there is considerable truth in these reports that are going about. I don't believe all I hear about the girl's beauty.'

'Oh, of course not,' said the Captain, inwardly chuckling.

'I dare say she is a pretty, dowdy doll; but when a man of my father's age makes a fool of himself, he does it with a vengeance. And if you were to speak to him seriously on the subject, he would ask you what business it was of yours, quarrel with you, and perhaps cut you out of his will, or turn you out of the house and forbid our marriage.'

'That would never do,' interposed the young gentleman warmly.

'No indeed, dearest Alfred,' replied the lady looking at him warmly and lovingly.

'What plan would you propose then my pet?' asked he, 'supposing that your governor does contemplate making a jolly jackass out of himself in his old age?'

'Well, Alfred, if he could be put out of conceit with the girl in some way – if he found anything against her character – something to disgust him in short–'

'I perceive,' replied Captain Torrant reflectively, 'but there is some danger. In the first place, proof may be very difficult to get to support the accusation; and in the second place any one setting such reports on foot would be liable to heavy damages.'

'Pooh, pooh,' replied Eliza, 'you have plenty of young scamps among your brother officers who would be delighted with the chance of taking a pretty girl's maidenhood. Only let me find out her address, and then you can give one of your friends the information, and let him make her acquaintance and seduce her; fuck her well, get her with child – anything – so that she is quite ruined and spoilt as to any purpose of becoming a stepmother to me.'

To this hopeful scheme, the gentleman assented, merely remarking that it would never do 'to trust any of our fellows with such a delicate business.'

'I see how it is sir,' exclaimed Eliza, 'you think that if there is any maidenhood taking to be done, you can do it pretty well yourself. And so you can, I can testify; only I think that your regard for me, that you profess so largely about, might keep you from straying after such a nonsensical baby-faced doll.'

'My darling Eliza, I did not propose to do anything of the kind,' replied the aggrieved dragoon, 'I merely said that I would not venture to entrust such a piece of business to any of our youngsters.'

'Ah well,' said the lady, 'I would rather have avoided this part of the business; but I suppose what must be, must; and if the girl is to be seduced and rogered, you will have to do it. Of course, it is all fun for you, but I can't help but feel a little bit jealous. You don't care for her I know, as you care for me, but still all you young reprobates like a little change, and I am told that she is fresh and rosy-looking, with golden brown hair; while as for poor me, I am sallow and colourless, and my black hair looks dismal – I know it does.'

We may presume that Miss Bonham made these remarks in full consciousness of her charms; for she really was a splendid woman. And of course her lover judiciously lost no time in informing her of the fact, accompanying his protestations with the warmest caresses. So that at last the young lady, fairly vanquished, promised to be no more jealous – than she could help; that she supposed Alfred would have to like Rosa a little – just a little bit – or he would not be able to seduce her; and that when that nice little bit of business was done, he must leave her in some gay house, or in keeping with one of his friends, or somewhere or other; Miss Bonham was not particular, only that Alfred must never see the girl again; and must marry her – Eliza – as soon as it could be managed, and then they would live happy forever afterwards, as the story book says. On this there followed more kisses and caresses, and the lovers went out for a walk in the garden.

Leaving them in their happiness we will follow Master Robert on his excursion to the Fieldings' farm; an excursion taken on his master's account as far as business was concerned, but not without an eye to his own amusement should opportunity occur. The day was fine, and he walked leisurely along, thoroughly enjoying the feeling of having got away from the barracks, and of having nothing to do; not that Master Robert was particularly over-burdened in that respect at any time. He had asked directions as to his road from one or two country louts, and was following a side path which bordered a wood, when he caught sight of some chimneys in the distance; this he thought might be the farm he sought; and while he was considering the matter he perceived in the adjoining wood a girl and a boy gathering fallen sticks. He spoke to the couple, desiring to know whereabouts Farmer Fielding's might happen to be. On this, the girl said her brother should show him the way, while she went home with the sticks.

But Master Robert, who had his eyes about him, and perceived that the girl, though coarsely dressed was a stout, buxom, fresh-looking lass of about seventeen, proposed that she should show him the way, and that her little brother should take the sticks home. The girl seemed to hesitate; but the boy being presented with a penny, cut the matter short by running off to spend it, and thus left Robert, as he wished, alone with the nice looking girl guide.

She was for going to the farm by the path, from which indeed, as she said, the house was easily to be seen; but Robert knew better than that, and said he was sure the wood must be a shorter way, and putting his arm around the girl's waist, led her along to where the bushes appeared to grow tolerably close. She laughingly declared that the way he was taking did not lead to anywhere; but did not seem to object nevertheless, even when Robert, spying a mossy bank, pretty well sheltered from observation, proposed that they should sit down there and rest awhile.

Finding that the girl was not at all ill-disposed for a little love making, though she might be a little shy, the jolly dragoon proceeded to seat her on his knee, taking the precaution in the first instance of raising her petticoats, so that he might have facilities for exploring her bare rump. And of course, when he had got her great fat arse thus comfortably established, he lost no time in shoving a couple of fingers up her cunt. As he found no maidenhead, he asked his rustic friend if she had any sweethearts among the country lads, to which she replied, smiling and shaking her head:

'No, no, Susan Flipper she had a sweetheart and she let him shove his cock into her, and she had a child and it gave her a great deal of trouble, – no, no sweethearts for me, thank you!'

'But what do you do, my precious, for something instead of a cock, and how do you happen to have lost your maidenhead?'

'Well, I don't know much about a maidenhead,' was the reply, 'but when I feel queer like, I get a carrot and ram it into me, into the slit between my thighs, that you've got your fingers in; and it makes me feel so nice – only one day I did it rather too hard, and burst through something and hurt myself.'

'Let's see,' said the astute Robert, as he turned the damsel over on her hands and knees, and pulling open the lips of her cunt, took a deliberate inspection, 'I can manage to give you a deal more pleasure than you can get from a carrot, Nelly (if that's your name) and without any risk of getting you with child.'

'Could you really now,' said the simple country girl. 'Is your cock quite harmless, then?' she asked.

'Certainly,' replied Robert, uncovering about nine inches of a wholesome looking and decidedly thickish prick, 'you perceive my dear, that if you go down on your hands and knees and I just shove in the red end of this machine, no harm can possibly happen to you: it is only when a girl is laid down on her back – with her thighs open, and her sweetheart gets atop of her and shoves the whole length of his tool up her that she gets big with child.'

'Ah, I know that's true enough,' replied Nelly, 'for Susan Flipper told me, that was the way her John got her down in the cow house, one day when she was milking, and what's more, she said he nearly split her arse up.'

'There's no fear of that with me, my pretty Nelly,' said Robert coaxingly. 'If you'll just go down on your hands and knees – on that soft mossy bank, I'll fuck you very gently, and will neither split your arse or get you with child.'

'Well, you are a nice looking civil young gentleman,' replied the rustic lass, 'and your cock is certainly an uncommon nice one, and a big one, – I only hope it is not too big, and so–'

'And so, I may! Isn't that what you mean to say, my pet?' interrupted Robert.

Then, taking consent for granted, he placed the strong well-shaped girl on all fours, with her jolly rump prominently stuck out, and the whole of her regalia completely displayed. As she was pretty tight, he at first kept tolerably well to his promise about not going further into her than the knob, but every shove made a difference, and by the time he had got to the fifth push, he was in up to the hilt, simply as far as his weapon would go.

Nelly did not reproach him greatly for his perfidy, on the contrary, she wriggled her bottom about, and even shoved it out to meet his furious lunges so that Master Robert enjoyed himself even more than he expected to do. That Nelly did the same may be pretty well inferred from the fact that when he was spunking into her, she was actually sinking under him with pleasurable emotion.

The young woman's first remark upon getting up was: 'Well now, I must get home to mother, or she'll wonder where I am. I don't know, young man, whether you kept very strictly to your word as to the amount of prick you just put into me, but I felt as if you put a deuce of a length! Howsome ever, it was all very nice; and if you should happen to be passing this way, some other time, I am generally somewhere about, and if you don't see me, any of the lads or lasses working hereabouts will be able to tell you where to find me. That is if you want to do so, because perhaps you think one go is enough, and you are tired of me already.'

Robert gallantly assured her that this was far from being the case, and took a most affectionate leave of her; at least, if giving her a crown piece to buy a new bonnet, while his fingers were groping about her rump, is a fair proof of affection on the part of the young man.

Then he pursued his way towards the farm house, which he never would have had the slightest difficulty in finding without any guidance; secretly congratulating himself that whether he succeeded or not, in doing any business for his master, he had managed a very nice little bit of amusement for himself. So far so good. Entering the farm house, he at once accosted a jolly looking dame, whom he correctly enough supposed to be Mother Fielding, asked permission to sit down and the favour of a drink of milk.

The old lady perceiving at once, from his neat plain groom's dress, and the cockade in his hat, that he was some superior gentleman's servant, and propitiated probably by his good looks, not only asked him to rest himself, but put before him a tankard of strong ale, and some bread and cheese, remarking that it would be hard if Fielding's Farm could not afford a tired stranger a mouthful of beer.

'Then this is Fielding's Farm, is it?' said the apparently astonished Robert, 'and you are the Mrs Fielding, mother of that beautiful young lady the officers at the barracks are always talking about.'

Mrs Fielding acknowledged that she was the mother of the young lady in question, not without a deal of conscious pride at hearing Rosa so described, remarking however that it was like the officer's impudence, to be so free in talking about her daughter.

'But I suppose,' concluded the old lady, 'it is all the same to them, my daughter or some body else's.'

'Truly madame, I fear you are not far wrong,' said the moral Robert, 'our young gentlemen are rather too free both in their conversation and manners, but in the case of so very distinguished a beauty, as I hear Miss Fielding is, little talk comes natural. Besides, madam, in this case it is quite excusable, as report does say that your daughter is going to make a high marriage.'

'People should mind their own business and not tell lies about other folk's affairs,' said Mrs Fielding, remembering Mr Bonham's admonitions on the subject of silence and secrecy.

'Ah, well, if it is a lie,' replied the astute Robert, making his point at once, 'I'll correct it – whenever I hear it – and mention my authority.'

'Not but what Rosa could be if she choose,' interposed the old dame, 'of course such things are generally unlikely.'

'Very unlikely,' here interrupted Robert, in order to interrupt her, irritate her and lead her on.

'But there are exceptions to every rule, and my girl Rosa, who is as good as she is pretty, may be an exception in this case. Mind, I don't say she is!'

'Oh, of course not!' interposed the military groom, 'and that's exactly the reason she has gone to London, I suppose!'

'Why, not exactly to be married,' replied Mrs Fielding, forgetting all about concealment in her own satisfaction, and drawn on by her guest's confident manner,

27

'not to be married just yet. You see, though Rosa has been well brought up, yet a little London polish is desirable to fit her for the high station she will occupy.'

'Oh, of course,' replied Robert, in a matter-of-fact way, as if he knew all about it, and highly approved, but thinking to himself all the while:

'You are a nice soft old lady, and if you let out this secret to every one as easily as you let it out to me, it will very soon be parish news. But your ale is good at any rate, so here's your good health, ma'am.'

This last remark was uttered aloud and acknowledged.

'Oh, I am afraid that you are a dreadful set up at the barracks, young man. You are in service to one of the gentlemen, I see. Pray, who may he be?'

'Only acting as officer's servant, madam,' replied her guest, 'you know the officers are at liberty to choose the smartest and best looking-ahem-of the men, to act as servants for them.'

'Certainly,' said the farmer's wife, 'why not? And who are you with at present?'

All this interlude gave Robert time for invention, so accordingly out he came with one of the biggest lies he had ever told in his life, – and that is saying a good deal.

'Major Ringtail, madam, of the 51st Dragoons, is the gentleman I am with. He drove over to Rutshole this morning, and as he did not want me to assist him in the business he was after, he gave me a holiday; which I thought I could not employ more innocently than by a walk in the country.'

'Quite right, young man,' replied the old lady, 'and what sort of a man is the Major?'

'Oh, he's a very nice quiet sort of a gentlemanly man,' was the reply, 'he's rather addicted to drinking and gambling, but then you know, Mrs Fielding, that officers at country quarters must amuse themselves somehow – and he may be said by strict people to be damnably given to cursing and swearing and fighting. Indeed, the Reverend Brother Stiggins said so the other day, when the Major kicked him out of the barracks yard. But then, you know, madam, men will be stupid and aggravating; and fools like Stiggins will interfere where they have no business. And people do say of my respected master, – people will talk you know – that he spends too much of his time in fornication; and that he is over much given to rogering any of the pretty country lasses, or any other girls that he may happen to fall in with. But I suppose that he considers that proceeding to be part of his duty, as an officer of HM's 51st Dragoons. And,' said Robert in conclusion, 'considering that he is a Dragoon officer, I think he behaves himself on the whole as well as can be expected.'

'On the whole' said Mrs Fielding to herself, 'well perhaps he does, I wonder how he behaves off the whole?' But she only said, 'Pray young man, what did the respectable gentleman, your master, kick the sainted Brother Stiggins out of the barracks for? I think that holy man was terribly indiscreet in venturing to trust his sainted body in such a den of iniquity. But I beg your pardon, young man, I did not mean to hurt your feelings, the words slipped out unaware.'

'Well, madam,' said Robert gravely, 'we don't generally call the barracks a den of iniquity. You see, perhaps our gentlemen might not understand what that meant, but it's commonly known by the name of Hell's Blazes; and Mrs Mantrap, the Colonel's lady, – his wife's at Cheltenham – calls it Little Sodom. But that's neither here nor there,' continued the narrator, with a side glance at his hostess's horror-stricken countenance, 'you were asking me about that little unpleasantness between the Major and that apostle Stiggins. I know all about it; for you see the Major had got me with him in case of Stiggins, or any of the congregation turning nasty.'

'What, were you in the chapel?' asked the old lady, in great surprise. 'And what were you doing there?'

'We were in Little Bethel Chapel, madam, to offer up our devotions to the best of our ability,' replied Robert demurely. 'You see in the tenth pew from the pulpit, on the left hand side, a deuced nice girl used to sit, and in the afternoon, generally by herself. I told my master, as in duty bound, and he was taken with a pious fit. So he found out who the girl was, and after speaking to her two or three times in the street, in the most impudent way, he pretends that she has converted him, – ha, ha! and says that he should like to be gathered into the fold, the only fold he was thinking of being the folds of her petticoats. Well ma'am, I don't think she could be quite such a fool as to believe all he said, but what with having her brain softened with Stiggins' nonsensical saintly trash, and what with the pride of showing off a Dragoon Officer as a brand: saved from the burning, in her own pew: and perhaps a little feeling of another kind besides, – you know what I mean, Mrs F – all combined together to induce her to make a fool of herself, and she made an appointment with the Major to meet her in her pew one Sunday afternoon, when her mother would be asleep at home and her father smoking his pipe. All this my master told me of course, for I was to stick to him, and what's more I got a special chum of mine, Tom Lieutenant Larkyns' man, to come with me and sit pretty close, for you see madam, there was no telling how the congregation, to say nothing of the deacons and elders, and that bad lot, might take it.'

'Take it! Take what?' exclaimed Mrs Fielding.

'Patience, madam, and you shall hear,' replied Robert with drunken gravity, for the strong ale was beginning to take effect upon him. 'During the first part of Stiggins' mountebanking, his prayers and howlings, and damning everybody except himself, up hill and down dale, my master behaved himself tolerably quiet, merely kissing Miss Larcher, (that's her name) every now and then, giving her an occasional squeeze, and putting his hand up her petticoats in a devotional manner, when they knelt down together.'

'Good Lord!' interrupted the farmer's wife, 'do you call that behaving quietly?'

'Very much so indeed, madam,' was the reply, 'not a sound was to be heard in the pig-market – I beg pardon – chapel – except the bawling of that Stiggins who bawled enough for sixty. His bawling had one good effect at any rate, it sent half his disciples to sleep before he got to tenthly and when he arrived and called thirteenthly, half the congregation were snoring comfortably. Not so my master and his fair friend. I had noticed him getting on very favourably. Once he laid her backward, on the seat, and took a regular good, long, groping feel at her privates. On another occasion he took out his standing prick and showed it to her; I suppose she wanted to convert that too, for she took hold of it admiringly. All this was very pleasant, and I suppose the Major had been keeping a pretty bright look-out on the state of the congregation, for when he perceived what I noticed, that one half of them were happily out of hearing of Stiggins' howls; he thought it a good opportunity to go to work in earnest. I had been stooping down below the level of the door of the pew to get a good suck at a flask of brandy and water, which I had brought with me to enable me to bear up against the fatigue and to bring myself into a devotional frame of mind, when on raising my eyes, the first thing I saw, was a pair of remarkably good legs, nicely set off by clean white stockings, and neat little shoes, showing over the side of the adjoining pew. Of course I knew what such an apparition as this meant, and if I couldn't guess, I was very soon enlightened, for on peeping over the edge, – as was my duty, in order to see that all was straight-forward and pleasant, there I saw my respected and gallant master fucking, as the common people call it, Miss Larcher in a most splendid style. The seat of the pew was not much of a rest for her fine broad rump, but in spite of her heavings and wrigglings, he pinned her hard and fast; and did not leave off until he had completely enjoyed her beautiful body. As for her, I only hope she enjoyed herself in proportion to her sufferings, for when the Major got off her, before she closed her thighs or put her clothes down, I noticed that her chemise was stained with blood, as she must have smarted a little.'

'But do you mean to tell me, young man,' interrupted Mrs Fielding, 'that none of the congregation noticed what was going on?'

'One of them did, Mrs Fielding,' coolly replied the narrator, 'but, as he came towards the pew, I told him it was the case of a female in a spiritual conflict with Satan, and that if he didn't go back to his seat, I'd make him and that damn quick. So, he went, apparently quite convinced. And as for the rest of the congregation, they were either asleep or stupid, as of course they naturally must be, to come to such a stinking hole at all! So my master buttoned his trousers in peace, and his pretty friend adjusted her dress, and they marched out, before Stiggins had nearly finished his yelling. But the brute from the top of his sentry-box, which he calls his watch-tower, had the advantage of overlooking the sleeping pens of his flock, and great was his disgust, as you may imagine, on perceiving a fine young ram like master, getting into the mutton of a pretty ewe lamb, like Miss Larcher. And he came to the barracks, firstly to threaten the Major with hell-fire, which he seems to know a good deal about, secondly to endeavour on finding the Major did not seem to care very much about the flames, to get a ten pound note out of him, by way of a bribe for holding his tongue. Then, on finding the Major did not care one damn whether he held his tongue or not, and did not propose to give him any money: he changed his tone once more, and told the Major that if he did not give him ten or fifteen pounds, he would tell Miss Larcher's father and mother, and would have her turned out of the congregation of the saints, completely disgraced. Upon this the Major informed him, that he, the saintly Stiggins, had been discovered in a pig-pen, rogering a young sow, that he, the Major, had half a dozen witnesses quite ready to prove it, and that if he annoyed him, or Miss Larcher with his blackguard lies, he would have him up before the magistrates for bestiality. And before the horror-stricken Stiggins could recover his presence of mind on hearing this intelligence, he found himself being kicked out of the barracks with speed and dexterity; and I have no doubt it did him a power of good.

'And now, Mrs Fielding, with many thanks for your kind hospitality, I must say good-bye. If you had another daughter at home I would ask for an introduction, but as it is, I must do without. Duty calls, madam, farewell!'

So saying the half-drunken Robert took his departure to report progress to his master, leaving Mrs Fielding lifting up her hands and eyes, as she exclaimed:

'Good Lord – a – mussy me!'

Chapter III

Considerable amusement was excited by Robert's recital of his conversation with Mrs Fielding. This, he lost no time in reporting to his master immediately upon his return; finding him in the garden, gracefully and agreeably employed in tossing his beautiful cousin about in a swing hung between two trees. The most important part of his story was relating to what the communicative old lady said about her daughter, and her journey to London, which at once confirmed Miss Bonham in her suspicions.

'Depend upon it, Alfred, the old goose has placed her in some good first-class finishing school, so that the future Mrs Bonham, confound her! may have a little surface polish.' (This was hitting the right nail on the head with a vengeance.) 'But,' continued Eliza, 'the deuce is in it if I don't find out either from her mother, or my respected father's correspondence, what her address is, and once found, I'll leave the rest to you, dear Alfred.'

As a further allusion to their plans before Robert, might be indiscreet, they changed the conversation; the Captain asking his servant if Mrs Fielding's ale was pretty good, and whether she had asked him who his master was. To the first question the hopeful young man returned a most unqualified assent: to the latter, he replied by giving his master an account of a certain Major Ringtail, to the Captain's intense amusement.

'And, upon my word, sir,' said Robert, 'it's just as well there is no such officer in the regiment; for while professing the greatest regard and attachment for him, I've given him a character that would damn a whole brigade, officers and men. The old lady's hair stood on end, so that it actually lifted her mobcap off her venerable head.'

'Why – what in the name of wonder, did you tell her, Robert?' asked Captain Torrant, who perceived his valet's half-tipsy predicament and anticipated some funny disclosures.

'Faith, sir, I could not tell you half what I said to her – not in Miss Bonham's presence, sir.'

'Oh, never mind Miss Bonham,' replied the Captain giving that lady a push to set her swinging, so that the colour of her garters was no particular mystery, 'she knows what soldiers are, and will excuse a little loose talk, so out with it!'

Thus adjured, Robert, who in his excited state wished for nothing better, started at once into his description of the gallant Major, while crediting him with every vice under the sun, or nearly so, and ending with giving him a character for high respectability, tickled Alfred's fancy amazingly.

Both he and his cousin Eliza were delighted with Robert's description of the scene in the chapel; and although the young lady actually did blush, and pretended to look confused, she swallowed every incident of the story with great gusto, from the appearance of the pretty legs over the side of the pew, to the mythical Major's withdrawal of his prick from its bleeding

35

sheath.

'How can Robert invent such a pack of nonsense, my dear?' appealing to her lover in pretended indignation.

'Indeed, my love, I think it is very natural and clever. I only hope that it is all invention. I say, sir,' (turning to his man) 'how did you come by Miss Larcher's name? Was that a name out of your own head, like the Major's?'

Here Robert, evidently a little confused, scratched the article referred to, as he said very slowly:

'Why, no, sir, not exactly. I was hard up for a name, and I noticed one as we came through Rutshole: Mary Larcher, sir, Temperance Hotel, sir. Little disreputable hole, left-hand side, High Street, sir.'

'My good gracious Heavens, Alfred!' almost shrieked Eliza, 'she is a most respectable woman, a regular prim, starched, old maid; and what's more, she's acquainted with Papa, and her being a regular member of Mr Stiggins' congregation will make the story seem as if it had some truth in it! And that abominable chattering old goose will go telling the story everywhere! Oh! how can you laugh so? It is very serious!'

This was addressed to her cousin, who seemed to think that this description of the maligned Miss Larcher, gave point to the joke; for he absolutely roared with delight, and went about stamping his feet in perfect ecstasies of enjoyment. It must have been contagious, for in spite of Eliza's vexation, knowing that the scandal must reach her father's ears, she began to laugh merrily, and even Robert, finding that his bringing forward a respectable woman's name was not going to bring punishment on him by his master – he cared for nobody else – indulged in a respectful snigger.

'It's all the same, sir, I suppose it don't matter much what I said about such rubbish as that there Stiggins?'

'Why sir?' replied the Captain.

'Only sir, that he went to the barracks next day.'

'You mean, you rascal, that you told Mrs Fielding that he went to the barracks,' interrupted his master. 'It's all the same, sir,' remarked Robert, coolly; and then proceeded to give his hearers an account of the Reverent party attempting to extort a bribe from the Fabulous Major; and that personage retorting upon the apostle with an accusation of his having been detected in the act of copulating with a pig. All this Robert related as he had told it to Mrs Fielding, with as much preciseness and gravity, as if he had been an eye-witness to the whole affair; copulating, kicking out of the barracks, and all.

Captain Torrant fairly shrieked and yelled with laughter.

'You'll be the death of me, you lying rascal!' he gasped out, 'you will, by Jove! Do you mean to tell me that Mrs Fielding swallowed this enormous bucketful of lies?'

'Well, I think she took it nearly all in,' was the deliberate reply. 'At any rate sir,' continued Robert, more cheerfully, 'if she did not believe it quite altogether, she is certain to repeat it all!'

'Your remark, Robert, is perfectly correct, and shows a knowledge of human nature, for which I did not give you credit. And now you can go and look after the horses; you have done more mischief during this forenoon than any other man could do in a month and I am perfectly satisfied.'

On this, Robert raised his hand to his hat, and turned to go, Miss Bonham calling out to him:

'And Robert, I'll trouble you to leave my maid Lucy alone, she is a nice girl, and I don't want her pulled about!'

Robert silently saluted, and took his departure.

'What a jolly row there will be all over Rutshole, won't there, my beauty? I can fancy I see Stiggins and

Miss Larcher, instructing their lawyers to bring actions against Major Ringtail or his man, or both for defamation of character! There is one good thing, the fact of Mrs Fielding being instrumental in spreading these reports won't raise her in the estimation of her future son-in-law!'

'That it won't,' replied Eliza, emphatically, 'and I think that Robert has done us a very great service this morning, both in raising these reports, absurd as they are, and getting us the information about Rosa.'

'Yes, he's a useful, clever fellow, but a dreadful scamp among the girls.'

'Takes after his master, I suppose!' archly interrupted Eliza, for which she was rewarded by almost being pulled off the swing to be kissed, while her lover thrust his hand between her thighs into her moistened cunt. Still keeping her in this pleasant position the Captain continued:

'What on earth did you tell him to keep off your maid for? Don't you know that it was the very thing to make him attempt her person?'

'Certainly not,' replied the lady, 'he dare not after my forbidding him, besides Lucy would not let him.'

'Oh, nonsense!' replied the experienced dragoon, 'if his prick begins to stand, he won't care for your forbidding him, or anybody else, and as for Lucy – to pay you off, my beauty, I dare say she takes after her young mistress!'

'Catch that for your impudence, sir!' said Eliza, giving him a slap on the face but not a very hard one, that's the truth.

'Well dearest,' said the Captain, 'I'll bet you anything you like that Robert fucks your maid within the present half hour!'

'Done sir,' was the ready reply.

And it was thereupon agreed that they should return

to the house to keep an eye on the interesting pair; Alfred lifting Eliza from the swing in such a way as to expose all the secret charms that young lady had to show, both to his delighted eyes and his searching hands.

'There, that'll do, dear,' said the lady reprovingly, 'no more at present, thank you! What shall our bet be?'

'Well,' replied her cousin, 'a younger lover than myself would bet twenty kisses, or a delicious fuck, but I am so blessed as to be favoured with those exquisite treats, nearly as often as is good for me. I'll tell you what your penalty shall be.'

Here he whispered in his cousin's ear something or other which the lady appeared at first to receive with high disdain.

'Nonsense, sir,' was her reply, 'you shan't do anything of the sort! My bottom indeed! most disgustingly indecent; and what's more, I do not see what pleasure I shall have in the matter. You will gratify your lust, of course, and very sensual lust it is in this instance; but I should think I shall be more hurt than gratified. Oh yes, I dare say my bottom is very white and pretty, but you are not going to enjoy it as you propose, Master Alfred, for all that.'

Now it was the Captain's turn and very eloquent he was. He represented that it would not hurt her at all, only tickle her; and as he would not have to use a condom, he should enjoy the unusual felicity of spunking into her.

'A special delight, dearest Eliza, from which in justice to you, I debar myself!'

'Well,' said the lady, rather relenting – 'you are a very good boy in that respect; and as you say you are quite sure you will not hurt me – to be sure, it is a horribly indelicate proceeding! But you are pretty sure to lose your bet, so the chances are that I shall not have to submit my posterior to any such indignity after all. And mind, sir, if you lose your bet, you are to bring me half-a-dozen pairs of silk stockings.'

'That I shall do – whether I win or lose,' replied the enraptured lover, squeezing his cousin's graceful waist, as they proceeded towards the house. As they went, they argued the point, as to where their faithful domestics were likely to be found; Alfred suggesting the stable or the hay loft as a likely place for a find, but as this involved the fact of Lucy going there to look after Robert, Miss Bonham repudiated the idea on behalf of her sex, and suggested a spare bedroom on the same floor as her chamber, as a likely place. Finally they came to the determination of visiting the stables in the first instance, and if unsuccessful there, of trying the bed-room.

On entering the stables, certainly there was no Robert. His horses were there, and all right, as the Captain at once perceived. Before leaving the stables however, he noticed an intelligent looking stable helper, busy with a broom, about nothing particular. To him the Captain presented a half-crown, asking him at the same time if the horses were all right, and if his man Robert, had been in the stable lately.

'Oh, dear, no sir,' said the lad, 'not for a quarter of an hour at least,' quite loudly, as if for the benefit of some third party hearing him; but at the same time he winked knowingly, and pointed with his thumb over his shoulder to an iron grating, which, as Captain Torrant well knew, divided the stable from the unoccupied loose box.

Unoccupied however, on the present occasion it was not, as the gentleman and his cousin very soon discovered. Proceeding very quietly in the direction indicated, while the stable lad made as much noise with his broom as he conveniently could, in order to drown any possible sound of their footsteps, the pair of lovers peeped through the grating and then their eyes were greeted with the prospect of another pair of lovers; and this was the position in which they were discovered.

On a loose truss of hay the elegant lady's maid, Lucy, was kneeling, with her thighs tolerably opened, while Robert, crouching down behind her, was imprinting lascivious kisses on her thighs, her rump and her cunt. Finally, confining his attention to the last feature, he divided the orifice with his tongue, working it about in such a way which must have inflamed Miss Lucy's amatory organs considerably. Then as he proceeded to take down his breeches, Alfred whispered to Eliza:

'Now, love, you see as he has ploughed up the furrow he is very properly going to put his seed into it – aye! there he goes – devilish nice legs, your little girl has got! Fine bottom too, very fine!'

'Surely, Alfred dear,' whispered his cousin, 'he cannot be going to shove his cock into her button hole!'

'No, dearest, I think not,' returned the gentleman, 'if he had intended to do so, he would have moistened that orifice and not her cunt.'

Captain Torrant was partly wrong and partly right. Robert certainly began in what is generally considered the legitimate sphere of action, but as Lucy was very much excited, and he had had already a very first rate fuck that morning, it so happened that the hand maiden arrived at the crisis of her enjoyment before the amiable young man had affected his share of the business. No doubt, in feeling her elixir bathing his cock, a bright idea struck him: he withdrew his weapon, and Lucy no doubt, fancied that he, like her, had finished his performance; so she made a slight movement, as if about to rise. But no such thing, mademoiselle! Robert put his hand to the orifice he had so lately occupied, and covering his fingers with her warm, oily liquor, dexterously lubricated her small rump-hole with it, inserting one of his fingers morever, as a light advanced courier, to prepare the way for that grandee – his prick. That noble plenipotentiary followed in due course, the only objection made by Lucy being such as may be expressed by a small exclamation of 'oh!' and a slight shrinking of her buttocks, as Robert's inflamed end forced its way into her small but elastic hole. And then the rogue seemed to enjoy himself thoroughly: his face absolutely glowed with lustful delight; and at every fresh thrust he gave, he made a low grunt, as a paviour does when using his rammer in the street. At last with one grand shove, he went right in up to the balls, and stayed in for about half-a-minute, motionless.

'Does that not look nice, my sweet Eliza,' whispered her lover. Eliza said nothing, but we suppose thought the more, and not altogether in a hostile spirit, it is to be presumed since, when her cousin again said, 'Now darling, while they recover themselves, suppose you come and pay me your debts,' she made no objection, but smiling and blushing, put her arm within Alfred's and allowed him to lead her out of the stable. The gentleman as he passed the stable boy, put his finger on his lips, which signal the discreet functionary well understood.

Then the lovers walked silently into the house, where however, a disagreeable surprise awaited them, being no less than the unexpected arrival of Mr Bonham!

'Oh, bother take him!' his dutiful daughter remarked, 'I did not expect him until tomorrow, or late tonight at the earliest. What can have induced him to return so soon?'

'Confound him!' muttered Alfred, apostrophizing his future father-in-law, 'what's to be done now?'

'Oh, perhaps now I shall get off paying my bet!' said Eliza, glancing wickedly at her cousin, then seeing the look of deep vexation that came over his face, she continued: 'never mind, dearest, he will perhaps want some refreshment, as it is still a good three hours till dinner- time, and while he is taking it, we can have another short stroll in the garden. There is a convenient little house of retreat, you know, among the bushes at the end of the serpentine walk, and there you know, although it is not a very genteel place for the purpose, you can–'

'Of course I can, darling,' interrupting her with a graceful kiss, 'what a capital manager you are!'

'Then mind, sir, that you are a good manager too,' replied the young lady. 'And don't hurt me any more than Robert did Lucy.'

'I shan't hurt you at all, pet,' was the reply. 'Robert was rather rough and piercing, I shall be very gentlemanly, only mind you bring a small pot of cold cream with you. A privy or a water closet is a capital place for such an encounter, as my injection might produce all the effect of a warm clyster.'

'Upon my word sir, this must be a nice treat that you have in store for me,' said Eliza, pretending to pout, 'but I have a little curiosity to find out a new sensation, and I suppose I must submit. Do you go back up to the stables, and warn the interesting pair whom we have just left, that our coachman will be coming in with horses, and I'll tell Papa that you have gone for yours, to be got ready for your return after dinner. Of course you have called here accidentally.'

So saying she slipped away.

Captain Torrant, going into the stables, called to the stable-boy, saying in a loud voice that his master had returned. This piece of intelligence produced Robert and Lucy pretty quickly out of the loose box, while the boy hurried out to open the stable yard gates, to admit the carriage. Lucy looked blushing and conscious, while Robert received his master's orders to prepare his tandem for their return at eight in the evening, with a most imperturbable expression of countenance.

'Please don't tell Miss Eliza, sir, that you found me with Robert in the stable,' pleaded Lucy.

'Oh, of course not,' was the officer's reply, thinking how unnecessary it was for him to say anything about it. 'I hope you have been enjoying yourself,' said he with a meaning look, and as she, covered with blushes, attempted to run past him, he caught hold of her and lifting her petticoats, exclaimed as he put his hand in her cunt. 'What a devilish nice pair of legs and thighs, and – ha! just as I expected, your nice little cunt open and moist! Did she make a good fuck, Robert?'

'Most lovely, sir,' with praiseworthy solemnity.

'Do let me go sir,' entreated Lucy, 'I hear the carriage coming into the yard.'

'Well, get along with you,' he said, 'I won't tell any tales, you may depend.'

'Thank you sir!' and off she ran blushing deeply.

'Governor come home, sir?' said Robert interrogatively.

'Yes, Robert, he has, and it's rather a bore, for he don't approve of my staying here all night – and if he does not invite me specially, I must go away at eight, but if it comes on to be a wet evening, I shall only drive as far as the Red Lion, in Rutshole, and go on to the barracks tomorrow. But you do be ready with the horses at eight, unless you hear to the contrary.'

Robert said, 'Certainly sir,' and his master walked into the house.

Here he met with a most gracious reception from Mr Bonham, – a couple of glasses of madeira after his drive, having put that gentleman into a rare good humour. He even bantered Alfred on his seizing the opportunity of his absence as a favourable occasion for calling upon his daughter Eliza; and he little knew – poor, innocent old gentleman – how near he was to the truth, when he affected to suppose that the young lady had given her lover notice of the house being clear. But Captain Torrant declared, with every appearance of virtuous innocence, that he came to consult his revered Uncle in supplying part of the purchase money.

This was so plausibly put, that, after some humming and ha-ing, Mr Bonham promised to take the matter into consideration. Then his fair daughter remarked, that as her Papa did not seem to have brought home any London news worth hearing, she would go and take a walk in the garden and of course Captain Torrant offered her his company.

'I'll join you in half an hour or so, my dear,' said her obliging Papa.

'Thank you, Papa,' said his grateful daughter, who could have dispensed with his company remarkably well.

'Have you got the cold cream, dear Eliza?' asked her lover, as soon as they were fairly in the garden.

'Of course I have, sir,' she replied, 'I don't want to run the risk of being split up more than is absolutely necessary, and although it is not becoming in me to be eager for such an abominable performance, still I should humbly recommend your getting your share of it over, before my respectful parent makes his appearance, for he might not seem to see it in the same light, and might even consider it somewhat remarkable, if he found us both coming out of the privy together.'

'You are quite right, as usual, my darling,' replied Alfred gallantly. 'And here we are, arrived at our little city of refuge – snug enough and not much fear of being interrupted. There is a bolt to the door I see. There now,' suiting the action to the word, – 'we are all snug, and you'll allow me to put you in the most convenient position.'

With this he raised one of Eliza's long graceful legs upon the closet seat, and instructing her to bend her head downwards, he turned her clothes over her shoulders. Then taking the cold cream from her, he not only lubricated her small orifice, but bestowed a plentiful supply of the emollient, over his eager cock, this time unsheathed and erect, in all the pride of naked beauty.

'And now, my lovely pet,' said he, laying the end of his cock upon the orifice.

But no sooner did Miss Bonham feel the rounded end, than a sense of great disproportion between his instrument and her hole became apparent to her mind, and she exclaimed:

'My dear Alfred, I do not wish to disappoint you, but I am afraid we have attempted an impossibility, you never can get into my body by this road!'

But the lustful young officer thought differently; he knew that if he could get one good inch well in – the rest was easy; and so, firmly but gently, urged his point; and was rewarded for his pains, by going into his darling's arse, with an easy gliding motion; the tight india-rubber-like elasticity of the passage being partially conquered by the copious application of the cream.

All that the young lady did was to mutter in broken sentences: 'So you have managed – it! dearest – I thought – you never would – be able! It does not hurt – me – as – I feared it – would – it only – rather tickles me. My good gracious! What a flood of hot oil you have injected into my bowels! Why Alfred dear, fond as you are of me, I think you never paid me such a lot of compliments at once, since we fell in love with each other!'

This last remark on the lady's part, was occasioned by the enthusiastic praises, lavished by her delighted lover on her various charms, as he was ramming his belly against the fine soft cheeks of her rump.

He seemed half mad with sensual rapture, and as well as his physical efforts would permit, kept up a running fire of expressions of admiration; in which his blind adoration mingled with good qualities of his mistress's mind and body together, in a most incongruous manner. He went on, in what would have been under any other circumstances, a most ridiculous way about her loving nature and her plump thighs, about her loving disposition and her delicious cunt; about her perfect taste in dress and her glorious buttocks, and finally referring to the delicious operation he was performing, declared that in all his experience he had never known such exquisite and complete enjoyment.

A good deal of this pleasure was, doubtless to be attributed to his lovely friend, who naturally flattered at hearing such enthusiasm exhibited with regard to her person, endeavoured to return the compliment by exerting herself as well as she could under what, to her, were rather unusual circumstances. All she could do was to straddle her legs as far apart as she was conveniently able, and to shove her rump out to meet her lover's long shoves. This she was the better able to do, as he did not perform nearly as quickly as she had been accustomed to be fucked when lying on her back, or in any posture with her belly up. On the contrary, he worked his prick in and out, as if he were desirous of protracting his treat, as there is no reason to doubt he really was. But he could not continue forever; and at last the interesting incident occurred, which called forth the remark from Eliza, about her 'bowels' and 'warm oil,' and etc., etc. Nor was this all, for when he withdrew his comely weapon from its charming sheath, and prepared to stow the much subdued implement away in the sanctuary of his trousers, Eliza remarked:

'Be quick, dearest Alfred, and get away with you, for to speak plain English, I want to make use of this little house in a necessary point of view.'

Indeed, before the gallant Captain could get himself buttoned up, nature compelled Miss Bonham, greatly against her ideas of delicacy, to lift the seat she had just been stooping over and again baring her beautiful bottom, to put the temple of refuge to its legitimate use.

All this the Captain viewed with the utmost complacency; in fact, he rather expected it, as a natural consequence, and was cool enough about the matter to hand his cousin some soft paper which he happened to have in his pocket. And there is not the slightest doubt that he would have waited in attendance on his fair lady, until she had finished her business, had not the prudent Eliza suggested the propriety of his absenting himself, for fear Mr Bonham should find him in or near the temple, which with Eliza inside, must have looked very suspicious.

So the gallant commander, lighting a cigar, took himself off and paraded a neighbouring walk, until such time as Mr Bonham should make his appearance, or his daughter should emerge from her lurking place. The former event took place first, and Mr Bonham's approach was made known by his heavy footstep, and his blowing his nose after the manner of a trumpet, heralding his advent.

'Ha! Alfred my boy, all by yourself! What have you done with Eliza?'

'Miss Bonham, Uncle, left me a few minutes ago, I don't know exactly where she has gone but I have no doubt she will return directly.'

The answer was made with the greatest coolness and most commendable gravity, and certainly without leaving the elderly gentleman room to suppose that anything uncommon had taken place during the last twenty minutes or thereabouts.

'Eliza is a charming girl, though I am her father and

perhaps should not say so,' remarked the old gentleman, as they walked along. To this, the younger one gave ready assent.

'And as good as she looks,' continued Mr Bonham.

'You should be no stranger to my opinion of my cousin Eliza's charms, by this time sir,' replied the young officer. 'I consider her to be all perfection, both in her mind and person (I wonder what the old boy would say if he knew how intimately I am acquainted with all parts of her beautiful body, both back and front.)'

This last remark, as may be imagined, he made to himself.

'Well, Alfred,' his uncle resumed, 'as soon as you get your step, I do not see any particular objection to your being married. What with your private property, your pay and Eliza's money – ahem! – you ought to be able to do very well, and I'll look and see what cash on hand I have at my bankers. I am not sorry to hear that your Major is about to leave your corps. I have heard a very bad character of him.'

'Indeed sir!' was the reply, 'I am surprised to hear that. Major Pobjoy is considered a very respectable man, rather pious indeed, and very discreet.'

'Pobjoy wasn't the name mentioned to me, but I heard of the affair this day, as I passed through Rutshole, and very hurriedly. A respectable tenant of mine, or rather the wife of a tenant,' (Mrs Fielding, I'll bet a sovereign, muttered Alfred) – 'told me some hardly credible stories about a certain Major named Ringdove, or Stifftail or some such name as that.'

'By Gad, she's very sharp about it!' muttered Torrant, and then said out aloud:

'I don't know any officer of that name, sir, but pray, what has the culprit been doing?'

'Why my dear boy, I hardly like mentioning such

49

indecent subjects; but I believe he had connection with a young lady of the Reverend Stiggins' congregation, in the chapel, under that faithful shepherd's very nose!'

'Pray, uncle, did the lady enjoy being fucked?'

'Why no, I can't say that I understood she did,' replied Mr Bonham, completely taken back both by the question and the straightforward way in which it was asked. 'But the scandal does not stop there, for on the sainted pastor proceeding to barracks next day to reprove the man of sin, and entreat him to flee from the wrath to come, Major Dovetail, or whatever his name is, accused the apostle of having been detected in the criminal action of having connection with a swine, and kicked him out of the barracks.'

'Had Mr Stiggins been discovered poking a pig?' asked Captain Torrant, with an air of great interest, not as if the incident was at all unlikely.

'Great Providence, nephew, no! Why Stiggins is next door but one to one of the holy apostles and–'

'But he may have buggered the pig for all that,' stubbornly insisted Captain Torrant, 'at least it is as likely as any part of the story. There is no Major Ringdove or Stifftail, or any such name in our regiment. One of the lambs of the fold may have got rogered, in the fear of the Lord, and in the middle of the sermon – very likely – and Stiggins may have been kicked out of the barracks, and may be again, if he goes there on any of his stinking errands. The pig copulation I know nothing about – I wasn't there so didn't see it. But here comes my fair cousin, so perhaps we had better defer our discussion until some other time.'

'I think so, indeed, Alfred,' was the reply, 'but I see that I have been imposed upon, and I should like to hear a little more from you on the subject, so instead of returning tonight, suppose you stay here and we will talk over matters in general, and your future prospects, matrimonial and otherwise. Here comes Eliza; let us walk together to the stables, and countermand your horses. . .'

So saying the trio walked off in the direction of the yard, Miss Bonham not at all displeased to hear her dear cousin's consent to pass the night at Rutsden Lodge.

Chapter IV

If Mr Bonham fancied when he asked Captain Torrant to pass the night in his hospitable mansion, that this gallant officer would content himself with the solitary wretchedness of what was generally known as the bachelor's room, we believe him to have been very considerable mistaken. Indeed Miss Bonham, by virtue of her position as mistress of the establishment, took the first step with regard to her cousin's comfort in ordering the best bedroom to be prepared for him. This the reader will recollect our noticing as being adjacent to her room.

The kind, thoughtful girl considered that if her dear Alfred were taken ill in the middle of the night, he would be so far away from any assistance she could render him, and, worse still, he might be afflicted with that terrible complaint known in the medical vocabulary as 'prickstand,' in which case he would be inconveniently far from her bed and a great deal too near Lucy's.

The result of this prudent arrangement was that the young dragoon did not occupy the luxurious bed allotted to him at all, but partially undressed, devoted half-an-hour to a fascinating book of a decidedly lascivious character. When that space of time elapsed, he made pretty certain of two matters; first, that his respected uncle was in bed and sleeping the first sleep of the just, and secondly, that notwithstanding his delightful encounters with his lovely cousin, in the course of the day, he was perfectly able to do her as much justice as she could possibly desire in the fucking department. Under this impression, he noiselessly glided from his room to Eliza's, the door of which, he quietly opened.

'Is that you, dear Alfred?' asked the young lady, neither surprised nor frightened; indeed the probability was that she had been expecting him, for she was wide awake and a dim lamp was burning in her room.

'Bolt the door gently,' she continued, 'and come to bed. You know after what Papa said this evening, I consider you as good as my husband now. But my goodness, Alfred, you have not got your sheath on, and how awfully stiff you are!'

To this the young gentleman made reply to the effect that he supposed the painful stiffness would be cured in a couple of minutes, and that with regard to the condom, as he expected his darling Eliza would become his wife in less than a month, that useful precaution was no longer necessary. The young lady assented, as indeed she would have assented to anything her lover proposed, and as he entered her luxurious couch, folded him in something more luxurious still, throwing her soft white arms around him, and placing one of her beautiful legs over him as he lay. We shall not detain our reader long in the lady's bedroom, as the lovers, being calmer than usual after the day's enjoyments, were disposed to be rational, somewhat in the manner of married couples after the honeymoon; so that the proceedings comprised a judicious amount of straight-forward fucking, variegated by alternations of refreshing slumber, enjoyed in each other's arms. But this quiet domestic sort of rogering, as it may be termed, is singularly effective in its results, though not as full of incident and excitement as more impromptu and passionate licentiousness – at any rate, one thing is pretty certain: that when Captain Torrant crept quietly back to his room about five o'clock in the morning, he had planted something in his cousin's garden, which bore fruit nine months afterwards in the shape of a fine boy.

After breakfast, the young gentleman mounted his tandem-cart, attended by his faithful Robert. On the sly he had taken the most loving farewell of Eliza, and without that secrecy, a most affectionate one of his uncle, who promised everything that was good natured, both with regard to his promotion in the service and his marriage to Eliza. All this was very agreeable to Alfred, although he certainly considered that his uncle's ready regard for his interest was partially attributed to his desire to get his daughter married and out of his house, before introducing a new Mrs Bonham as mistress thereof. But whatever the cause, the experienced commander sensibly reflected that it was his duty to take advantage of his uncle's liberality while he could. Serenely turning these matters over in his mind, he arrived at the barracks, where he was welcomed by his brother officers, with whom he was a decided favourite, each in his own peculiar way. The Colonel, in a polite, man-of-the-world style, hoped that he had had a pleasant visit, and wanted to know when he might be presented to Mrs Alfred Torrant. The Colonel did not like his officers to marry except with wealthy and handsome women; money of course was an advantage in the regiment, whoever it belonged to, and the Colonel liked pretty women – maids, wives and widows; so as Alfred bade fair to acquire both advantages united, the Colonel wished all success to his suit. Major Pobjoy remarked that it was not always that a young man had a prospect of so many worldly advantages, together with the blessing of a regenerate father-in-law. To which Alfred – who did not care much about the Major, as he was leaving the corps, – replied that he did not know what a 'regenerate' meant, but if it meant religious, his venerated relative was a devilish good fellow, but rather too strong on that point.

'He read us an epistle, or a chapter, or something last night, Colonel. He did, I assure you,' said Alfred, addressing his superior officer. 'The first epistle of Saint Jeroboam to the Rechabites, or some such people, and it was all I could do to live through it, thought I should have yawned my head off – upon my word I did.'

Thus saying, the Captain toddled off to his quarters, out of hearing of the irreverent comments of divers of his younger comrades, some of whom opined that if Torrant was not married to Miss Bonham, the sooner he was the better, while one of the lot Julius Larkyns, gave it as his opinion that Alfred looked as if he were married already.

A shrewd remark – founded upon Alfred's subdued appearance – for which our readers who have borne that young gentleman company during the past twenty-four hours, will feel disposed to give Captain Larkyns credit. This gentleman with one or two others of the same kidney, were speedily summoned to a conference by Alfred, he being suddenly smitten with an idea that a messenger might be very shortly expected at the barracks enquiring for Major Ringtail, in order to serve him either a summons before a magistrate, or to deliver him a lawyer's letter, threatening an action of damages for defamation of character.

And as Captain Torrant had nothing to do until he received Rosa's address from Eliza, it struck him that it would be a pleasant and profitable method of spending his leisure time, if he and his companions in arms were to get somebody to impersonate the Major, and thereby get some fun out of the victimized Stiggins, and the unfortunate Miss Larcher. Words are faint to describe the delights expressed by the young officers of HM's 51st Dragoons on hearing such an agreeable game proposed to them; and their respect for their friend's henchman, Robert, as a mischief-maker, liar and blackguard generally, amounted to something very like reverence. But it would never do to let him personate the Major, for he might be brought into contact with Mrs Fielding and be recognized, but as one of the lieutenants piously remarked:

'Thank God there are plenty more scamps in the corps, and we shall find one clever enough to impersonate the Major or anyone else for that matter.'

The first thing to do was to warn the sentry on duty not to refuse anyone admittance who came asking for Major Ringtail, the second thing to do was to dress up Julius Larkyns' man in a shooting coat belonging to that gentleman, and arranging that he should occupy his master's quarters, as soon as Stiggins or any of his missionaries made their appearance.

This was not very long in happening, for Larkyns, who was smoking a cigar, with his head out of the window, suddenly exclaimed:

'Here he is! That must be him, I'll go and direct him up here. You stay here you fellows!' addressing Torrant and three or four more, 'you are only keeping the Major company in weed, you know!'

So saying off he went, and his friends followed the idea, saw him accosting a fat, bloated, palefaced unwholesome looking man, who seemed staring about half-bewildered in the barracks yard. Under the kind pilotage of Captain Larkyns the doubt was soon solved, and the hapless Stiggins entered the room of the so-called Major Ringtail. On entering, Captain Larkyns gravely addressed his man Tom with:

'Sorry to intrude upon you Major, but this party was looking for you, and I thought it was well to bring him up to your quarters.'

'Quite right, my boy, as long as he isn't a dun,' readily replied the soi-distant Major.

'I am no dun, sir,' answered Stiggins, intending to be majestic, but rather taken aback upon seeing what a knot of daredevil looking youngsters he had intruded among. 'I am a minister of the word, sir, an 'umble apostle of the truth sir, and my name is Stiggins!'

'Oh, indeed!' was the cool reply, 'sit down, Mr Stiggins, glad to see you – you're the man that buggered the pig, ain't you? Interesting zoological pursuit, I should imagine! Julius, mix a little refreshment for Mr Stiggins, he must be thirsty after his walk.'

The pious man half rose from his seat and essayed to speak, but he could not. He stuttered and gasped, and his eyes rolled in his head, while his pasty looking face became purple. While he was thus endeavouring to give vent to his indignation, Captain Larkyns adopted the hint of his quick witted man, made him some 'refreshing' drink. He got hold of a rum bottle and half filled a tumbler, then he was going to administer a trifling modicum of water, but Torrant took the jug away and gave him in its place a bottle of gin. A portion of this added to the rum made a cool wholesome mixture; the flavour being slightly modified by a lump of ice, three or four bits of sugar, a piece of lemon and some nutmeg. To this fearful compound, Larkyns gave the impromptu title of 'The Prince's Mixture.'

Gravely addressing the almost convulsed preacher, the young officer said:

'You seem rather unwell, reverend sir, wearied in body and somewhat troubled in spirit, perchance? Pray allow me to adopt our worthy Major's suggestion, and offer you a slight refreshment. It was considered a valuable stomachic by that model of all the monarchs – the late George the Fourth – named Prince's Mixture, in his honour when Regent.'

'Under those circumstances, young man,' replied Stiggins, majestically, 'I shall lay aside the conscientious scruples which I entertain against drinking anything but the water of the brook; but being in duty bound to reverence the powers that be, I feel myself called upon to follow the example of the august monarch you have named.'

Hereupon, reducing his features to something like a human expression, he took a pretty fair pull of the dangerous compound; remarking, as he placed the half emptied tumbler on the table, that it was somewhat potent.

'Not at all,' replied Larkyns, 'it is only your Reverence's water drinking habits that make you fancy everything else strong in taste.'

'Truly it may be so, but my business here is with Major Ringtail,' replied Stiggins, turning to address that individual. 'There is a terrible story spread abroad sir, to the effect of my having been seen in an unseemly position with a swine, and that you have been heard to accuse me of that indiscretion without any consequences resulting on my part, and I have come here not only to put a stop to such abominable reports, but also to demand satisfaction in some shape or other. Indeed, I consider it due to myself as a preacher of the word, to have amends made to me in a pecuniary sense, for the damage my character has sustained.'

To this exordium the so-called Major made no reply, but Larkyns quietly slipped a wine glass full of Scotch whiskey into his reverence's tumbler, while Torrant coolly said:

'I presume Major, that your friend here is the party who was accused of fucking the old sow, in Farmer Codson's pig-stye?'

'Nothing of the sort sir! It's an infamous falsehood!' shrieked Stiggins, rising from his chair and stamping in high wrath.

'Take it easy, my friend, take it easy,' continued Alfred, 'anybody may be mistaken.'

'Oh certainly!' interrupted the mollified pastor, taking a big drink.

'And if you preferred buggering a pig to fucking a sow, I don't see that it is anybody's business!'

Here there was another outbreak on the part of Stiggins, drowned however by the roars of laughter following Alfred's peace-making amendment. All that could be distinguished was a heap of broken sentences, such as:

'Go to magistrates – bring action – defamation c'racter – spectable lady member cong-g-ration, Miss Larcher, thousand pounds damages!'

'Silence, gentlemen, if you please, a lady's name is mentioned! Let us be cool and hear all about it!'

This was from Captain Torrant.

'And take your drink, Mr Stiggins,' said Julius, 'have another lump of ice in it?'

'Not because you tell me, young man,' replied the holy man in an offensive tone, 'but because I am a free agent and shall do as I like.'

So saying, to the unconcealed delight of the young scapegraces, he took a little more rum and another lump of ice. Then being anxiously pressed by the Major to know if he had any fresh accusation to make regarding Miss Larcher, he began such a rigmarole about the Major having fucked that much injured lady, and not having done so, and only spreading a lying report to that effect, and that he had never been kicked out of the barracks – not he indeed! – he would like to see the pig that would fuck him out of barracks; and he would bring an action against Miss Larcher, that he would.

'I presume the long and short of the story, Mr Stiggins, is that you fucked Miss Larcher,' said Captain Larkyns, continuing with an appearance of great interest. 'Well, I never did roger a girl in chapel myself, during divine service, but I have no doubt there is a certain piquancy in it. Did she make a pretty good fuck, Stiggins? Had she a fat arse?'

There is no telling what answer that sainted man might have made in return, for drink and indignation had made him half mad. But the question was immediately started whether it was not the pig who committed himself with Miss Larcher in the chapel, and one of the young sinners bawled out one thing and one another, till the whole question of the pig, Miss Larcher, the chapel, Major Ringtail and the barracks was involved in chaos. One thing was plain enough, Stiggins was drunk.

Then arose the question: what was to be done with him? Finally, it was resolved to adopt Captain Larkyns' views. He suggested that their respected victim would be in a state of total unconsciousness, and that a strong solution of gum, if glue or tar could not be had, should be applied to the sainted countenance, and that some feathers, taken from the pillow of Cornet Periwinkle, as the officer who had joined last was known, should be distributed, so as to give the holy man the appearance, as nearly as possible of an owl. That being the bird of wisdom, was hailed as combining amusement with compliment, if the Reverend Stiggins could only be brought to view it in the same light. Then the apostle should be placed on a wheelbarrow, with his saintly mug enveloped in a sack, lest peradventure, the eyes of carnal men being cast upon him, scandal might be the result; or what the young dragoons were much more afraid of, the order of the procession might be interrupted in some way.

Major Ringtail, divested of his master's shooting jacket, was ordered forthwith to go and find a wheelbarrow, and a country lout game enough to wheel a load to the Temperance Hotel in Rutshole. Yes, dear reader, that was where the Reverend Stiggins was going, to the much-maligned Miss Larcher's Temperance Coffee-House; he, her much revered visitor and pastor, being in three predicaments – in drink – in a wheelbarrow, and in the semblance of an owl!

During Tom's absence, his master and his master's companions betook themselves to adorn Stiggins, with as much earnestness and business-like gravity as if they were doing the most praiseworthy act in the world. One of them concocted a note purporting to be from his Reverence to Miss Larcher, containing expressions of attachment and an offer of marriage. This, neatly folded and addressed, was placed between his right thumb and forefinger, these articles being lashed tight together, greatly to his Reverence's comfort no doubt.

Towards dusk, according to orders a wheelbarrow and a grinning country lad were in attendance outside the barracks gates; the youngster being promised half-a-sovereign if he performed his errand satisfactorily, and one shilling and a licking if he mismanaged matters, readily undertook to convey the apostle to the private door of Miss Larcher's hostelry, there empty him out, and ring the bell as if the place was on fire.

Moreover three or four of the gentlemen present undertook to walk in the same direction, in small but separate parties, so as to watch the result; and also to give aid to the countryman, in case of his conveyance or its interesting freight being interfered with by impertinently curious people, or any such disagreeable interlopers.

Then Stiggins was borne forth and deposited in his chariot: the conductor thereof upon being questioned as to whether the load of sanctity would not be rather too much for him, replied in the negative, asserting that he had barrowed many a heap of 'mook' as doubtless he had, and in the same barrow too – very lately.

'So,' as Mrs Hermans says, 'the stately march went on.'

Torrant and Larkyns were about twenty yards ahead on the side path; then, in the middle of the road came the body of their victim, watched by Tom, walking carelessly along the path abreast the barrow; then two more officers.

Robert begged his master to let him take part in the procession, but it was considered dangerous.

When Rutshole was reached, these precautions showed the wisdom of the prudent young men who had adopted them. For the vedettes, if we may use the expression, encountered a policeman, who was staring with some curiosity at the conveyance moving slowly along the High Street. He was immediately collared by Larkyns and Torrant, humbugged by an impromptu story of a lost pocketbook by Larkyns, and escorted to the 'Red Lion' to talk about the matter, over a glass of brandy and water. So the coast was clear, and the two gentlemen of the rear guard arriving immediately reported that the barrow was in the act of depositing its precious freight.

Immediately there was a rush made for the door, when the conductor was seen bowling his empty machine down the street on his homeward journey at a devil of a rate.

Simultaneously there arose from the opposite side of the street a shrill scream. The policeman and the officers immediately hurried across to render what assistance they could, most probably – and also perhaps to see the fun.

There they found Miss Larcher, her waiter and two housemaids in agonies of screaming at a prostrate figure, the upper half of which was enveloped in a sack, which the animal inside whatever it might be, was endeavouring to get rid of – but in vain. We are bound to say that the two young officers upon arriving at the scene of action, did not devote their first attention to the writhing tenant of the sack. They knew all about that kind of thing – but Julius nudged Torrant, saying:

'I say, Al, is that Miss Larcher? I thought she was an elderly piece of goods.'

'Well,' said his friend, critically, 'so she is, certainly, one of the has-beens! I should say: forty or nearly so, but still I agree with you, she is a fine well-made sort of an old girl, well kept too, I shouldn't wonder. Devilish good fetlocks, she has got!'

This interesting comment referred, as the reader will perceive, to the general appearance of Miss Larcher, who was by no means the starched old maid that Miss Bonham, in her conversation with her cousin implied her to be. She had decided remains of former good looks, and, as Alfred's acute eye had remarked, very neat ankles, judiciously clothed in neat kid slippers and black silk stockings.

'Toss you up for her, Alfred!' suggested Captain Larkyns, in as commonplace a sort of way as if it was a bottle of wine that was in question.

'Oh, no, my dear fellow,' replied his friend, 'you are quite welcome to try your luck.'

'Then don't you interfere,' said Julius.

'On the contrary, my dear fellow, I shall be happy to assist your virtuous endeavours in any way that I possibly can. Shall I curry favour with the lady by ordering a couple of gallons of coffee, and a bushel of buttered muffins? That's the sort of thing to do her I suppose?'

'Ha, ha,' laughed Julius, 'in half-an-hour's time, if I have any luck, you may have a buttered muffin or bun either if you like!'

While this confidential interlude was going on, the policeman, assisted by the waiter, had been dragging at the sack. This was removed at last with some difficulty to the operators, and more pain to the patient, as some of his glued on plumage came off in the operation. Still there remained enough to make him look 'a thing of beauty,' which one of our poets remarked, 'is a joy for-ever.'

We presume that it was from some deficiency of poetical temperament that none of the spectators, always excepting our military friends, could see the adornment of the Stiggins mug in this light. At any rate, Miss Larcher screamed, and her maids yelled. The lit-tle waiter stood in speechless awe, and the policeman remarked in a musing tone:

'Well, I've seen a good many rummy stares but this beats all I ever did see. Suppose 'e must a been an' got drunk, an' slept in a 'en roost.'

'Drunk, the disgusting brute is certainly,' interposed Captain Larkyns, who was a three bottle man.

'But he must not lie here, disgracing a respectable lady's house,' said Alfred, backing up his friend.

'Then I shall get a stretcher,' said Bobby, 'and have him taken to the station.'

'No, don't do that,' said the considerate Julius, 'or else Miss Larcher will have to appear – as a witness before the magistrate – most disagreeable position for a young lady to be placed in.'

'You are always right, Larkyns,' replied his faithful friend. 'I say, Officer, never mind saying anything at the station. Take the degraded beast across the street to the Red Lion and tell the boots from me to find some sort of a bed somewhere. I'll pay for it. He can be turned out when he's sober, you know, and there'll be no trouble to you, and no nuisance to Miss Larcher.'

That lady simpered and smiled, and expressed her sense of the polite consideration of the two gentlemen, and finally asked them to step in and refresh themselves. This being exactly what Julius wanted, the two friends were preparing to enter, when all of a sudden Captain Torrant pretended to discover that the object of their united disgust had a folded paper in his hand. This he extricated from between his finger and thumb, not dreaming however of severing the ligature that bound them together. And then gravely addressing Miss Larcher he remarked:

'By an extraordinary coincidence, this note seems to be addressed to you.'

'To me!' exclaimed the lady in great surprise, tearing it open, and in the first instance looking at the signature:

'Seth Stiggins! Why it can never be! Yes, but it is though – oh my, what a state for a babe of grace, a minister of the word!' Then, looking into the contents, she continued: 'Oh, the nasty, filthy wretch, take him away – out of my sight – such an insult! Into the nearest horse-pond with him,' and so on, in a high state of wrathful excitement.

Here the policeman returned with a couple of men and a stretcher; and Captain Torrant paid them all three for their trouble, while reiterating his commands to have the culprit conveyed to the Red Lion.

In the meantime, Julius was accompanying Miss Larcher to the house, begging her most earnestly and affectionately not to agitate herself.

'Indeed sir, you are very kind and polite,' replied the lady, 'but to think of that wretch, whom I have so long considered one of the elect, coming to my house in a filthy state of intoxication, and with a face like a badly stuffed owl, and to deliver me such a note – oh, I shall die of shame and horror!!'

'Not at all, my dear Miss Larcher,' replied Julius tenderly, 'we cannot afford to lose you on account of any such a wretch as that. Pray what is in his vile scrawl that should agitate you so deeply?'

'Indeed sir, I am almost ashamed to show it to you, but here it is. It would have been bad enough if he had written it while tipsy, but he had been sober enough when he wrote it, and that makes it more insulting, I know his handwriting.'

Here Julius could hardly keep his countenance, for the note had been written, partly under his direction, by Cornet Periwinkle. It stated in effect, that as she, Miss Larcher, was tolerably well provided in the world's goods and he Stiggins was not, he would have no objections to save her character by marrying her. That his friend, Major Ringtail, had told him that she made a most delicious fuck; as indeed he himself partly guessed from seeing the way in which she tossed up her pretty white legs and doubled them over that gallant officer's back, when he was rogering her in the pew last Sunday; but as he, Stiggins, considered that locality too much exposed, he suggested the vestry, after divine service, or indeed the sofa in her own private apartment, as a more suitable spot for the consummation of their mutual affection. Concluding with a philosophical remark that she needn't be shy, for he had ascertained that the dimensions of the Major's cock were so huge that she needn't be afraid of one of a milder description.

Upon reading this precious production, Julius rose with a grave face, went to the door and locked it, glad of the opportunity of turning his back upon the lady, to conceal a triumphant grin that would come upon his features. When he returned, his face had resumed its gravity as he remarked:

'My name, dear Miss, is Larkyns, a Captain in the same regiment as this Major Ringtail, and I assure you I shall call him to account for his abominable slander.'

'And then he'll shoot you, Captain Larkyns,' exclaimed the lady, clasping her hands together in an agonized way, for the young gentleman's handsome face and figure had begun to produce a great effect upon her.

'Perhaps he may, dear Miss Larcher, but in the cause of injured beauty and innocence, I can dare anything, and if I fail you can drop a tear to my memory.'

On this artful speech, Miss Larcher (who had not been made love to for some years) turned on the Captain a look so full of love and gratitude, that the young gentleman who was by no means troubled with bashfulness, passed his arms around the lady's waist and pressed his lips to hers, murmuring as he did so:

'Make me your champion, my darling, and I will dispel this vile slander or perish in the attempt.'

To this magnificent speech, Miss Larcher could only mutter something about bloodshed, and never seeing him again. Then Julius, as if a bright idea had struck him said:

'Perhaps this villian of a Major will retract and confess it is all a lie. It is a lie, I suppose, my darling girl, is it not?'

'Oh, Captain Larkyns!' she exclaimed, in a tone of reproof.

'Nay,' said he, hastily, 'I believe it is a lie, but to make other people believe; that's the thing. There is one proof of the incorrectness of the story – that the wretched Stiggins talked about your white stockinged legs over the side of the pew. Now that part of the story is evidently false as I perceive you wear black silk.'

'Certainly,' said she very readily, 'of course, I always do,' and at the time displaying more of her legs in corroborating her statement than in prudence she ought to have done.

'Oh what exquisite legs!' said the artful dragoon, kneeling down and commencing to kiss them.

'Do you think so, Captain,' replied the lady smiling and blushing.

To this there was no verbal response, but there was more extensive kissing, in both senses of the word, higher up (he had got to her thighs by this time) and stronger in quality. And then Julius, as quietly and slyly as the operation would permit, insinuated his hand between the lady's thighs, and his finger inside her cunt.

'Oh, Captain Larkyns,' she sighed, 'I am learning to love you. Do not destroy my self-respect.'

'My sweet friend,' Julius astutely replied to this, 'I am your champion for life and death; permit me to assure myself that when I give the slanderer the lie to his teeth, I shall be speaking truly and conscientiously.'

To this the lady made no reply, but a heavy sigh. Perhaps she was soft enough to believe the seductive Larkyns; perhaps she had a longing for something, she knew not what. At any rate she was fairly in for it by this time, and made no resistance when Julius laid her back on the sofa, with one of her legs over the back of it, and the other supported by a neighbouring chair.

'This is the sofa, I suppose, on which that brute Stiggins proposed to violate you, my darling, but from henceforth it shall be kept sacred as the altar on which you sacrificed your sweet person to your devoted lover Julius!'

'Ah, Julius,' said Miss Larcher, as the dragoon was raising her clothes and opening her thighs, 'be gentle with me, indeed, I am inviolated and free from the lust of man, do not hurt me.'

'I respect you as much as I love you,' replied the lying

scamp, taking out his long stiff prick, and saying to himself as he did so, 'what a jolly tight fuck the old girl will make! Here goes for her maidenhead the very first shove!'

And indeed it was so, or very nearly. Before making the shove, he took care to have himself very well established, and then when he did make it, there was a scream, not that Julius cared, for he knew that his faithful friend, Alfred, would keep intruders out of the room. He persevered in his vigorous shoves, until Miss Larcher, reassured by his passionate words and burning kisses, forgot the smart of the pain, and tasted something very like pleasure – and when Julius injected his spunk into her, and sank into her arms, she experienced a feeling of satisfaction from the sentiment that he belonged to her now and would come and ride her again. She was right there, and not far wrong in believing Julius – she would believe anything he said – when he assured her that he would have Major Ringtail turned out of the regiment next day. She little thought how easy it was to turn a man out of the regiment who was never in it.

Leaving Captain Larkyns to congratulate himself upon knowing where to go for some fresh cunt, when the spirit moved him, and Miss Larcher to take what pride she could in the idea that if she were not a married woman, she was at any rate no longer an old maid, we will follow Rosa to her finishing school at Mrs Moreen's.

Here, as may be expected, a parlour boarder like Rosa, met with a good deal of consideration. A few showy accomplishments, and a fashionable deportment, were all that she was required to learn, and naturally lady-like and clever, their acquisition did not cost her much trouble. But she was destined to learn some other accomplishments at Mrs Moreen's establishment, such as that worthy lady probably knew nothing about, and which she certainly never charged for in her half yearly bills. For instance, it is usual among young ladies of Rosa's age when thrown a good deal into each other's society to form close alliances, bonds of everlasting affection and so on. Then ensue confidential communications about lovers, cousins and brothers, revelations as to secret longings, and the liberties which the dear little creatures have permitted to that naughty boy, Harry, or that darling Frederick, and so on. And in the young ladies' bedrooms the descriptions were sometimes illustrated, particularly as when in Rosa's case her bedfellow was her most intimate friend and confidante, Miss Harriet Lovit. This young lady, who was a few months younger than Rosa, was a thorough adept in all sorts of licentious practices. On the very first night of their sleeping together, she clasped Rosa in her arms and tried by getting between her thighs to excite her lust, and produce something that a young gentleman in the same position would not have failed to produce. But though Rosa had no objection to the proceeding, and stretched her thighs as wide as she could, and kissed her newly-found friend affectionately in acknowledgement of her well-meant efforts, the only effect produced by their two tender young cunts rubbing together, was to make the pretty pair long for something else, something which was not at hand.

'What are you two girls doing there?' asked Charlotte Arden, one of the occupants of the other bed, in a sleepy voice.

'I am trying to fuck dear Rosa,' said Harriet plaintively, 'and I can't manage it so as to make her spunk.'

'Of course you can't,' was Charlotte's prompt reply, 'it is only one woman in fifty who has her clitoris prominent enough to produce the desired effect upon another woman's cunt, and for a girl like you the thing is a sheer impossibility. Shove one of your fingers into her and frig her well. She is very ungrateful indeed if she does not perform the same kind offices afterwards, for you.'

That Harriet immediately acted upon this sensible advice, may be inferred from the fact of Rosa beginning very shortly afterwards to sigh, to spread her thighs open right across the bed, and finally to clasp and kiss her bed fellow in a transport of delight, murmuring broken sentences expressive of gratitude, and finally covering her two fingers and her knuckles with warm spunk.

'Have you done her business, Harriet? And has she a maidenhead?' asked the young lady from the other bed.

'That I have nicely,' was the reply, 'and she has a maidenhead, really and truly.'

'Oh, upon my honour,' exclaimed Charlotte, 'that state of things will never do. I'll take it for her with a candle; we can't have any maidenheads among girls of our age, in this establishment,' continued she laughing.

'You shan't do anything to her tonight, Charlotte, I can tell you that!' said Harriet, 'she is very well frigged and does not want anymore at present. Besides you goose, if Miss Downey' (the second governess) 'were to find, on her inspection of the rooms tomorrow morning, our candle, stained with blood, there would be a pretty to do.'

'Miss Downey is not a bit better than any of the rest of us,' replied the other young lady. 'When she was in the garden privy the other day, I peeped through the key-hole and saw her ramming a huge carrot into herself until I thought she was going to have a fit, and I know that Signor Loretti, the Italian Master kissed her and felt her, on the stairs a day or two ago.'

'That is all very well, and likely enough,' responded

the prudent Harriet, 'but it would not prevent her from reporting us to Mrs Moreen, if she found any suspicious signs and tokens. Besides how do you know whether Rosa would like to have her sweet little virgin treasure violated by you and your candle? I should think that she would very much prefer me to take it.'

'Oh, yes, dear Miss Harriet,' exclaimed Rosa affectionately, 'I don't think you would do anything to hurt me, and if you were a young man, I would allow you to shove your cock into me as much as you pleased.'

'What is the child talking about?' interrupted Charlotte. 'What does she know about cocks?'

'I have seen my guardian's – Mr Bonham – ' replied Rosa, simply, as if it were the most common place affair in the world, and her guardian had only been doing his duty in displaying his jolly tool, and attempting to roger her in the carriage.

'Good gracious, your guardian's prick? How was that? How did it happen? Tell us all about it.'

Such was the chorus of exclamations that broke forth, and Rosa promising that it was a great secret, delighted her room companions by relating the trifling circumstances that took place during her journey to London in her respected guardian's carriage.

Then came a running fire of cross examination, something as follows:

'Wasn't it delicious when he put his tongue in and licked your cunt? Was his prick a large one? Did you take hold of it? Did he hurt you when he shoved it into you? How much did he spend in you? Wouldn't you like it again?' and so on; all of which Rosa Fielding answered to the best of her ability, and apparently to the satisfaction of her friends, who showed their sympathy with the proceedings by a certain degree of restlessness in bed and sundry long drawn sighs and 'Ahs' just as if they were tasting or fancied they were tasting something very nice.

Indeed Miss Lovit gave a practical proof of the excitement the short story had raised in her bottom, (and private parts) by altering her position in the bed, and placing her lovely bottom over Rosa's face, so that her cunt rested on the sweet girl's mouth, and her face, by this manoeuvre, of course brought upon Rosa's lately moistened orifice.

As she did this she begged Rosa in a most coaxing tone to thrust her tongue into her feverish cunt, and to lick it, and roll it about therein, just as Mr Bonham had done to her. The good natured girl at once complied, and really, for a novice, managed this difficult office to perfection, as the lascivious Harriet, already excited by frigging her new friend, was brought to the verge of spunking by Rosa's simple narrative, and the latter had not licked and sucked the gaping orifice for more than a minute and a half, before Miss Lovit began to interrupt the grateful licking she was administering to Rosa's quim, by various licentious and pleasurable exclamations, such as:

'Oh, you sweet girl – you darling! That's right! suck my clitoris! I wish your tongue was twice as big! Oh that's it! Go on,' etc. etc., concluding by a long drawn sigh, as she covered our heroine's face and half filled her mouth, with a delicious ejection of warm spunk. Of course with such capabilities and loving inclinations to accommodate themselves to each other's wishes, the two young ladies became fast friends.

Rosa had very little more to tell, but her more experienced friend found great pleasure in dispelling her ignorance and charmed Rosa, particularly by describing with great gusto, her first experience in the fucking line, and the loss of her maidenhead.

'We had a large Christmas party, last year, my dear Rosa, and my mother requested my brothers, who were then at home, to bring as guests, two or three handsome young eligible men of their acquaintance. This they had very little difficulty in doing, as one of them being at college, and the other in the army, they knew plenty of handsome young men, capital partners in a waltz.

'Or,' added Harriet, consciously, 'in any other amusement. I really believe, vanity apart, I was looking very well and my brother John who is intended to be a clergyman, and who is the naughtiest fellow I ever saw or heard of, seemed to take some pride in introducing his particular friend, Mr Melville, to me. He also, it appears, was destined for the church, and conducted himself accordingly. I supposed there is something in the prospect of wearing black, and preserving an outward appearance of respectability, that induces young gentlemen similarly circumstanced, to conduct themselves like young bulls, or lively rams; at any rate they generally do so. On the present occasion, my brother John, introducing his friend to me, said in a whisper, which he hardly cared to make inaudible:

'Stunning girl, I can tell you, Harry, she has the finest and longest legs of any girl of her age you ever saw!'

'For shame, John, hold your tongue,' I exclaimed, blushing scarlet.

'All right!' said he, laughing, as he went away, leaving me with Mr Melville.

'Now I must acknowledge that I had permitted Master John to take sundry improper liberties with me. I considered at first it was very wrong in any young man, unless he were an engaged lover, to take up a lady's petticoats and feel her cunt and bottom, but John assured me that it was quite a family matter, and further demanded, if a brother could not take liberties with his own sisters, who was he to take liberties with? This line of argument might not have been altogether approved

74

of by my Mother and Papa, but we carefully concealed our little interviews from other eyes than our own. He it was who initiated me into the mystery of frigging. He really gave me a great deal of pleasure and I used to do my best to show my gratitude by chafing his white cock until the spunk used to fly off in a jet nearly a yard from him. And he used to do even worse than this.'

'Why surely,' interrupted Rosa, 'you never allowed him to get into you? That would be very wrong I know.'

'Not in the way you mean, my dear,' replied her friend, 'though, really, if he had attempted it on some occasion when he had excited me with his finger I do not know how I should have been able to resist him. But however, he had too much prudence, whether I had or not, and confined his devotions to my small orifice.'

'Do you mean your bottom-hole?' asked the wondering Rosa, 'I should have thought it was too small altogether!'

'So I should have thought at first,' was her friend's reply, 'but it really is not so. A little ointment, or hair oil, and gentle shoving for the first minute, and then it becomes a very nice operation, delightful to the gentleman and not at all objectionable to the lady. There is nothing so bad but what some good comes of it; and these proceedings of my favourite brother, though I must consider them improper, had the good result of making me very particular in my person and dress, especially in regard to my underclothing.

'John used to say that he used to detest a girl who wore her hair bedecked in the height of fashion, and wore necklaces and jewels, and had a dirty cunt and bottom. Next to this, one abomination, he declared, was a twenty-guinea silk dress, concealing a dirty chemise and drawers and slovenly gartered stockings. It's a pity that girls more generally speaking, are not aware of the very strong opinion held upon this subject by the opposite sex; at any rate on this occasion I had reason to congratulate myself upon being particular. How many waltzes Harry Melville danced with me I cannot remember, but I have good reason to remember breaking my sandal towards the latter part of the evening. This dreadful accident had to be paid immediate attention to, and we withdrew from the dancing room to the stairs for this purpose, but, Heaven help us, whether any other ladies had been breaking sandals, or loosening their garters, I could not tell, but the first flight of stairs was thickly populated. Harry proposed that we should adjourn to the second flight, but I hardly liked this, as it seemed rather too brazen an operation. As I hesitated, John came up and addressing Melville suggested the propriety, with some cheerful slang, of an adjournment for bitter beer purposes. But my gallant partner would not have it so, for the present, at all events, and put the fracture that had taken place in such a terrible point to view, that John, who knew that a couple of minutes' attention from one of the servant girls would set all to rights, pretended to take the calamity in the light that his friend did, and suggested his study and smoking room – chiefly the latter – as a harbour of refuge. As he said this he chuckled to himself, but did not offer to accompany us, as we both, knowing the way perfectly well, proceeded to the sanctum in question. Here I seated myself in John's lounging chair, while Harry turned up the gas and bolted the door. These proceedings I pretended not to notice, as demurely stretching out my silk clad foot, I awaited Master Melville's proceedings. These were at first simple enough, he drew off my satin slipper, took out his penknife and deliberately cut away the broken parts of my sandal. These he coolly pocketed, remarking that he would retain them – as a keepsake. But his next proceedings were not so cool, before putting on my shoe, he

76

covered my foot with kisses, from my feet he proceeded to the calves of my legs, and even higher, and as he had taken care to locate himself between my legs, he was favourably situated for making further researches.

'Even with your very slight experience, my dear Rosa, you can imagine the exciting nature of my situation. I knew that my handsome admirer was doing what is commonly called wrong, and that I was to say the least of it, guilty of indiscretion, but still when he began kissing my legs and shoving his hand under my petticoats; with his fingers gently separating the tender lips of my cunt, I could not help stretching my thighs open, no, not for the life of me. The consequences may be easily imagined. He altered his situation a little, taking up my clothes with him as he arose and dropping his trousers to his heels, he imprinted hot, lustful kisses on my lips. Then standing a little way off me, he raised his shirt and taking one of my hands, laid it upon his Lordly priapus. I eagerly clasped the great, stiff, throbbing machine and felt so eager for its insertion, that I had neither fear of the operation nor dread of the possible consequences. You see, Rosa dear, that I have a sensibly sized mouth, not a little bit of a rosebud as you and some of the other girls have, and it is almost always the case that when a girl has a useful sized mouth, that her cunt corresponds to it in dimensions. Besides I have had the advantage of many a luscious fingering and licking from Master John; so that when Harry guided the end of his mossy tool in between my mossy portals, I felt no pain until the hot plum-shaped knob came against my virgin barrier and then I exclaimed, 'Oh, my dear Mr Melville, you are hurting me!' But instead of drawing back, he pushed into me with renewed energy, laying his hot lips to mine and murmuring. 'Will you not try and bear one minute's pain for my sake? My darling girl, do not drive me out of Paradise!'

'This was said so lovingly and enthusiastically, that I did my best to reciprocate his ardour; so, raising his shirt, I clasped my silk-clad legs, which John had recommended over his naked back, and shoving forward his rump, did my best to meet his thrusts half way. Between our joint efforts, my maidenhead, as you may guess, vanished like a cob-web, Harry ejecting his semen well up me, almost at the very moment of his successful penetration. Very fortunately for me, the pain of the operation checked my inclination to spend at the same time, or the consequences might have been serious. Nothing less than a swelled belly, I am convinced, would have been the result!!

'You have never been properly fucked, yet, my dear Rosa, but let me give you a little bit of advice. However good and kind your guardian may be to you, you will never have the same intense pleasure in yielding to him your virginity as if he were a handsome young lover. I cannot convey to you an idea of the kisses, the embraces, the vows of eternal affection, which were lavished on me by the enamoured young man, as, still retaining his position, but without exerting himself, he lay with his cock still soaking in its lacerated orifice. He specially recommended the purity of my skin, and the great taste and care bestowed upon my underclothing.

'Even when he drew out of me his limp and dripping, but still swollen cock, he did not cease his praises, but bestowed bountiful kisses upon my bottom, body, legs and thighs. I must confess that I was sorry to see him begin to button up, because the first momentary pang having been got over, and the passage having been well lubricated by his spending, I thought that a second edition of his proceedings might let me have my share of delight. How reckless a girl is, Rosa, when once she gets her animal passion fairly inflamed! The men are held chiefly to blame in most cases of rape and seduction, but upon my word, I think they have generally more consideration for our sex than we have for ourselves.

'I mentioned to you the precautions taken by naughty brother Jack with regard to my rump, when I declare that I could have hardly refused him entrance into the other orifice if he had attempted it, and now on this occasion, when my endearing expressions, lingering kisses and sighs, told Harry Melville all too plainly that I wanted him, in plain English, to fuck me again, the dear self-denying fellow told me that he must take proper precautions or I should certainly find myself in the family way. He proposed to visit me on the following day, and to provide himself with certain sheaths, made, as he described them, of some very delicate fabric, so delicate indeed as to be imperceptible to me, which would however prevent any serious consequences, even if he fucked me a dozen times a day. The dear fellow smiled joyously as he announced this fact, and I blushed, but more with pleasure than shame. The next thing was to arrange where to meet, and we finally settled that if we found it impossible to have a few quiet minutes to ourselves at my home, I should walk out to the library, or some other equally eligible spot, and meet him, at the residence of a highly respectable old lady, who professed to keep lodgers, but who had a kind and feeling heart for young people in distress and want – of each other.

'But we did not immediately feel the necessity of this hospitable arrangement; for instance, two days after our ball Mr Melville called, and after a little ordinary polite conversation with my mother, said he would take the liberty of waiting for my brother John in the study, as that young gentleman had made an appointment to meet him at that time. My mother was going out for a drive in the park, and I announced my intention of putting on my bonnet and going out for a short walk. To this my mother assented and shortly afterwards took her departure, when I went upstairs. But I did not reach my bedroom, as passing the door of John's study the door partially opened and I saw my lover peeping out.

'Time was precious, so that he murmured my name in appealing tones and I lost no time in entering the room; where I was instantly clasped in his arms, and he forthwith bolted the door. After a few kissing preliminaries, he forthwith took out of his pocket-book a semi-transparent sheath, with which he covered his beautiful standing prick. This being done, he applied a little ointment procured from one of my brother's drawers, and really at a little distance it was impossible to tell that he had any safeguard on at all, then placing myself against the wall as he requested, I put one of my feet upon a chair, while he took my petticoats up. My inspection of his cock and the sheathing process, had raised my expectations and my clitoris, to a remarkable extent, and the position I was in, though rather hard to sustain, is certainly one where the lady gets the full extent of the gentleman's powers. In this instance, though I did not feel the pain of a lost maidenhead, I was nearly lifted off my legs. Still the inconvenience of this proceeding did not prevent my experiencing the most exquisite pleasure, and I bathed my admirer's hair at the root of his weapon, before he arrived at the crisis of his enjoyment. This was but the prelude to numberless encounters of a similar description, always more or less ecstatic, both in my brother's study and at the respectable and convenient lodgings, kept by Mrs Boss. But pleasure cannot last forever, and I had to return to school while Harry had to go back to college. Before we parted however, we renewed vows of mutual affection; he, on his part, declaring his intention of marrying me as soon as he could see his way clear towards anything like a settlement in life, and I faithfully promising that however good my offers might be, received in the meantime, I would wait for him.

'Now, whether anything will come of the matter, I know not,' exclaimed Miss Lovit, in an amusing tone. 'He may fancy somebody else better than me; or circumstances may compel me to marry for money, but at any rate Rosa, to finish my story, I can tell you that I have enjoyed myself very much, and without any harm being done.'

This narrative pleased Miss Fielding very much, the prospects of enjoying the ecstasies described by Miss Harriet without running any risk of becoming big with child, on any favourable or tempting opportunity, was very delightful. Then Mr Bonham's attachment was a certainty, whether he made her his wife, or kept her as his mistress, he would not have taken the trouble and expense of placing her at Mrs Moreen's for no purpose.

Consequently, she was very much pleased upon receiving a letter from Mr Bonham about a week afterwards, in which he announced his intention of visiting her to see if she was happy and comfortable. He had, he said, informed Mrs Moreen of his intended visit. That lady, on the day indicated, gravely recommended Rosa to go upstairs and change her dress, and to make herself look as becoming as possible. The good old lady had not lived sixty years in this world for nothing, and knew that the better Rosa looked, the better her self-made guardian would be pleased, and the more Rosa was indulged, the better account she would give of her situation, and the more likely she would be to stay out the year, or two years, whatever Mr Bonham designed. Consequently when Rosa was sent for into the drawing-room to see Mr Bonham, with whom Mrs Moreen had already had some interesting points of conversation, she was looking so very blooming and handsome that the older lady evidently considered her a credit to herself and her school. And then she withdrew politely, considering that the guardian and his ward might have some interesting family matters to talk over. And Rosa did commence the conversation, by enquiring as in duty bound, how her father and mother were. This question being answered satisfactorily, her worthy guardian proceeded to take her upon his knee, which proceeding Rosa rewarded by giving him an affectionate kiss. Thanks to the conversation and fingerings of Miss Lovit, and one or two other young ladies, our heroine was not nearly so bashful as she had been during the incidents in the carriage, and thought that if Mr Bonham was a little encouraged, she would be mistress of an establishment of her own, and no longer a school girl all the sooner. So when Mr Bonham began gently to raise her clothes, instead of remonstrating with him, or offering to prevent him doing so, she said in a coaxing tone:

'I hope my dear guardian, you are pleased with my appearance, Mrs Moreen told me to dress myself as well as possible and to make myself look nice, and I hope – oh, if you want to inspect my silk stockings and underlinen, you are quite welcome. You ought to, for it is due to your great kindness that I look so well. Had you not better bolt the door?'

This last speech was produced by her respectable lover beginning to show signs of virility. He had got the forefinger of his right hand in his protégée's cunt, while with his left hand he was trying to free his manly weapon from its imprisonment, but he was in too great a hurry to taken any such precautions as bolting the door. If he thought at all on the subject, he no doubt considered that Mrs Moreen knew better than to come into the drawing-room again. If so he was right.

But whatever he considered, it is quite certain what he did, that was to shove Rosa backwards upon the sofa, requesting her to pull her clothes up and stretch her legs wide, while he let his trousers slip down to his knees and tucked up his shirt. As he carefully inserted the purple end of his respectable tool into the young girl's little quim, she said in whispering tones:

'Oh, my dear Mr Bonham, recollect that I am still a maid, no one but you has so much as even attempted my virginity, and if to give you this pleasure, I suffer pain at present and loss of reputation in future, you will keep your promise, won't you, and make me your wife?'

By this time the worthy gentleman had got well into her, and she was so deliciously tight, so sweet in all her private parts, and her face was so blushing and beautiful – that if she had asked him to make her Empress of China, he would have sworn to use his best endeavours in that direction. As it was, he stuttered out as well as he could, for he was ramming through her virgin barrier, that she should be his wife in twelve months, if he could wait so long for the full enjoyment of her lovely person. It must not be supposed that he made this honestly intended purpose coherently, for it was much interrupted by his gallant efforts to penetrate into his ward's sweet sanctuary, and also by soothing her, and stopping her mouth with kisses to prevent the half-uttered exclamations which Rosa could not entirely repress. At last, he managed to get in, up to his balls; and in two or three more shoves experienced the delight and relief of spunking into a virgin womb. He sighed with satisfied pleasure, as he sank with his whole inert weight upon Rosa's belly and breasts, telling her that she had charmed him beyond anything that he had imagined possible, and that he would come to see her again as soon as prudence for her sake would possibly permit.

All this was very pleasant for Rosa to hear and made up in some degree for the smart caused by her burst maidenhead. This however her experienced protector assured her could easily be alleviated by the use of a little luke warm milk and water. And so making her a present of a pretty purse containing a sum for pocket money, and complimenting Mrs Moreen upon the improved manners and appearance of his ward, he took his departure.

That very afternoon, however, as he was strolling towards his club in Pall Mall, somewhat to his surprise, he met with Captain Alfred Torrant, of the 51st Dragoons. That young swell attributed his presence in London to having some business at his army agents; and as this was natural enough after the conversation he had had with his uncle, the pretext passed without challenge; the facts of the case, however, being that Captain Torrant had treacherous designs against his worthy uncle, intending if possible to find through this means, some opportunity of introducing himself to Rosa, and also not adverse, upon a suitable occasion, to offering to lead his relative's elderly boyhood into snares.

This trap the good Mr Bonham did not fall into at once, as he announced that he was going to dine at his club, so Alfred declared, prompted by a bright invention, that he and a brother officer were going to dine at Greenwich, and proposed that they should call for him a* the Fag and Famish Club, and go down the river and dine together.

This suggestion was at once adopted by Mr Bonham, as being a very good one, and the three carried out their project. Mr Bonham brought with him a country appetite, and perhaps felt the want of a stimulus to supply the natural exhaustion caused by his exertions that morning. He ate heartily and drank deeply, more deeply indeed than he was aware of.

Such stuff as champagne and Moselle and claret,

could not take effect on such a port-wine drinker as he was, he thought.

Couldn't they though? more especially when consumed upon top of cold punch, pale ale, Madeira all of which beverages he had partaken since dinner began. So that when a return to London was proposed, the worthy gentleman felt quite regenerated, physically speaking, and 'up to' any species of amusement proposed by the young officers.

After a little consultation with his friend, Captain Torrant confidentially informed Mr Bonham, that if he would promise not to tell Eliza, he would show him a scene or two of London life known only to a few of the initiated.

'All right, Alfred my boy, I'm game for anything,' was the reply.

So upon arriving at London Bridge, two hansom cabs were chartered for the friendly trio. One four-wheeler would have held them all – but catch Captain Torrant riding in a four wheeler except with a pretty girl inside, and even then with the blinds down, so his fashionable friends could not witness his degradation.

We did not hear the direction given to the drivers, and so cannot specify the exact locality of the establishment to which their course was directed; suffice it to say that at the end of about a half hour, Mr Bonham found himself at the door of a respectable looking but rather dingy house, in a quite out of the way street.

On the young officers presenting their cards, the party was instantly, and most graciously received by a stout, smiling and gorgeously dressed lady, who did the honours of a gorgeously and handsomely furnished room, provided with what Mr Bonham considered a superabundance of luxurious sofas.

More champagne was immediately the order of the evening, and Mr B having been introduced to the hostess as a gentleman of high standing in the country, that lady politely inquired of him if he would like to see some of the handsomest girls in London, completely stripped, or only in partial deshabille, as with the semi-transparent skirt of the ballet dancer, and nothing else.

Captain Torrant immediately proposed that the young ladies should exhibit themselves in a state of nudity, all but slippers and silk stockings; but his friend, Lieutenant Archer, declared himself for a short, a very short skirt. There was a certain charm, the gallant officer averred, in taking up a girl's dress, however scant it might be, and perhaps he is right.

The prudent Mr Bonham, agreed to leave the matter in the hands of his more experienced young friends, and fancied he had done quite right in doing so, when six very handsome girls were introduced; three being dressed, if their skirts can be described under such an appellation, according to Mr Archer's idea, and the rest delighted Captain Torrant's ideas and eyes, with the exhibition of their beautiful forms, perfectly nude.

There was every variety too, tall and short, plump and slender, brunette and blond vying with each other in the display of their ravishing limbs, buttocks, bosoms and private parts.

Our readers will probably be astonished at Mr Bonham's apathy when he saw his daughter's accepted suitor, his future son-in-law, take one of the naked girls up in his arms, seat her on the edge of the table, open her thighs, and the lips of her cunt, and then, with her legs supported over his shoulders, begin to ram into her, as if the great object of his existence had been to shove his cock through her up to the roof of her mouth. Nor was Lieutenant Archer one whit behind his friend in taking advantage of the delights by which he was surrounded. True to his creed, he knelt down behind a tall, lithe, dark haired ballet-dancer, and alternately kissed her milk-white rump and her well preserved and scrupulously clean orifice. Then placing her on her hands and knees on the floor, he dog-fucked her, to the intense admiration of Mr Bonham, whose middle-aged prick began to glow and stiffen, as it had not done for many a year.

We can easily imagine that every movement of his person and every glance of his eye, was eagerly watched by the four disengaged girls. At length a plump little one, a ballet dancer, impudent as little people are wont to be, came and perched herself upon his knee, and commenced kissing him with admiration, genuine admiration too, no doubt, for she had been told that he was rich, and was a jolly looking bird enough. But one of the sisterhood was bolder still. She was a tall, brown-haired girl, good-looking enough, but not strikingly handsome as the other girls were. Perhaps on this account, her mossy sanctum had been less worshipped, and she felt the want of a few inches, or yards – as the case may be – of wholesome cock. Be this as it may, she knelt down before Mr Bonham, and, no doubt, to the disgust of the little lady who had taken possession of his knee, deliberately opened the front of his trousers, and released his cock: stiff and swollen up to the bursting point, from its irksome confinement. Determined to carry out her idea successfully, she not only chafed the interesting stranger, but sucked him gently; this established her advantage over Maria, – the little girl on his knee – for the effect on the excited gentleman was such that he hastily called out:

'For God's sake, don't do that! or I shall spunk into your mouth!'

And arising from his seat, he kissed Maria, whispering;

'You next, my little pet!' and laid the tall brown haired Emily on one of the purple, velvet-covered spring sofas.

Short lived indeed was his joy. Emily held the lips of her mossy treasure open: at one single thrust he was in her up to the balls, two more shoves on his part, two upward heaves and a convulsive wriggle of the rump of the highly accomplished Emily, and it was all over, for the time being, at any rate, and the highly respected Mr Bonham, of Rutsden Lodge, lay with bare rump and soaking prick, exhausted in the arms of his lascivious enchantress, in the presence of eight much edified spectators, male and female.

Chapter V

The two remaining girls and Mrs Goater, the mistress of the establishment, were not entirely idle spectators of this delightful proceeding. They began to take advantage of the champagne and cold supper, oysters and other provocative delicacies, displayed on the side board; and while enjoying these, they passed laughing comments on the pretty tableaux, which were being performed around them.

One of the lasses indeed, a French girl, called Coralie, had been a special favourite with Captain Torrant, and probably only missed being first fucked on this occasion from the circumstances of her being arranged in about five and twenty inches of skirt and silk stockings up to her rump, whereas, as we have seen, the gallant commander's tendencies on this occasion were in favour of nakedness.

This girl, we say, exhibited her attachment towards her former admirer by slapping his buttocks, kissing and rubbing his balls, inserting her finger into his hole, and making use of other little endearments, which clever girls, and French girls particularly, consider serviceable in raising and renovating a man's lusts.

We hardly suppose, by the way, that the young gentleman required any such stimulant, but however, he was duly grateful, and when he drew out his drooping and dripping prick, he rewarded the lady with a lascivious kiss, and a groping feel which explored her secret recesses in most effectual style. An adjoining bedroom supplied the means of ablution to the participants in the luscious games, and then they all set down to supper. We might prolong this chapter ad infinitum were we to describe the eating and drinking, and the lascivious conversation that went on, but we must confine ourselves to the most striking incidents. One of these was that Maria, who no doubt considered that it was high time for her to have something to do, collared Mr Bonham's cock and by frigging it gently, endeavoured to induce it to regain its perpendicular station. But notwithstanding the oysters and wine, and other more direct incentives to lust, Mr Bonham was not able as yet to stiffen so as to be serviceable. Our readers will readily understand what we mean, when we say that a middle-aged gentleman as he was, may have the desire for an immediate repetition of his joys, but be unable to raise his virile member up to the altitude which ladies consider as their due. On this occasion, he begged Maria to wait a little, but the young lady was evidently afraid lest someone else should cut in before her, as Emily had done, and deprive her again of the benefit, not only of Mr Bonham's prick, but of his pocket. So she fondly whispered to him that if he would allow her, she would raise a prick stand for him in two minutes.

Mrs Goater, who only partially heard this conversation, but who, (experienced soul!) guessed what was going on, proposed the operation of a birch rod, but Maria rejected the idea, for the present at any rate, but that the rod might be serviceable at a later period of the night. So saying she made the moral Mr Bonham lie down on his back, on one of the luxurious couches; then taking his shirt up and breeches down, she put his virile member in her pretty, soft mouth, as Emily had done. The effect was almost immediate: the gentleman's dormant powers were raised, his tool slowly lifted its head and began to fill Maria's mouth. When the clever girl perceived that her operations were successful, she requested her lover to remain in the position he then occupied, and placed herself astride of him, à la St George. In this way she certainly saved him every trouble, for she grasped his tool, inserted it, settled her weight down upon him, thereby admitting the whole length of it into her pretty little person, and began to work up and down in the most effectual and delightful way. And Mr Bonham was just about to spunk, when he was temporarily stopped by a proceeding which astonished him a good deal more than Maria, who had probably seen the same operation performed more than once.

His surprise was due to Lieutenant Archer, who had been contemplating the movements of Maria's lovely bum with evident pleasure, and at last could not resist the tempting object any longer. He made his advances very cautiously, both for fear of startling and disturbing Maria, and from a charitable dislike of disturbing the interesting rite which was being celebrated.

But he did it – yes, he did! Administering some saliva upon the girl's small, yet not altogether maiden orifice, he gradually, and with gentle pushes, insinuated the head of his instrument and then the rest was easy. He slid in – up to the root of his plant.

Looking over Maria's shoulder, he cheerfully addressed the prostrate Bonham with:

'How are you going on, old fellow? Jolly, eh! I'll take all the trouble off your hands, and Maria's too. I'll shove her down upon you! You like having two pair of balls banging against your arse, don't you Maria?'

But Maria was speechless. Whether she thought the more, or whether her attention was so completely absorbed, by a duplicate application of prick, she knew best herself, but this was certain: she exerted herself to the utmost, and earned well deserved praise from both her admirers, who injected their copious jets of warm cream into her as nearly as possible at the same time. On the conclusion of the operation Mr Bonham exhibited some curiosity to know how his pretty partner liked the bum-hole part of the entertainment, remarking that it was quite a novelty to him.

'What, my dear sir, and you a lusty widower!' exclaimed his dutiful nephew, Alfred Torrant, 'I should have thought that when you were the husband of such a splendid woman as my late Aunt, that you would not have neglected making trial of such a luscious performance.'

'Well, I must own,' responded the elder gentleman, for wine and lasciviousness made him speak out, 'that I did try on the little game more than once, but then I never took proper precautions. Had I gone deliberately to work and anointed my weapon properly, I might have succeeded, but the only occasions when I dared venture upon it, were when Mrs B was asleep, or pretended to be so, and then it took such immense shoving and exertion to get the knob of my tool in, that she awoke, if indeed she were ever asleep, which I rather doubt, and then she was angry, and declared it was the sin of Sodom, and a lot more nonsense of the same kind, for she was a very pious woman, so that I was obliged to turn her over and give her a jolly good fucking, only for the sake of peace and quietness. Though it is my belief,' continued the worthy gentleman, in a musing tone, 'that if I had got fairly into her, I should have had no scolding, or heard any balderdash about Sodom, or any other place.'

'Dear me!' exclaimed the graceful Emily, 'I am quite

surprised! I thought that married men knew everything, – that they were up to every move, as the saying is.'

'It just depends upon what sort of a bachelor life they have spent, my darling,' replied Captain Torrant, 'if they have spent a "good boy" humdrum sort of existence, the chances are they make but stupid companions for their young brides, who I am sure, must have either the trouble frequently of enticing them, and instructing them in their duties (which I have no doubt plenty of them are able to do, by the bye) or else go without their lawful gratification. And as for any married ladies calling any such innocent little gambols as we have just been carrying on, "unchaste" why, it is all nonsense! A pretty thing it would be indeed,' continued the young officer in a state of righteous indignation, 'if a husband could not get into his wife, how, when, and where he liked."

'Certainly, Alfred,' responded Mr Bonham, nodding, 'I quite agree with you.'

And in his present frame of mind he was quite sincere, and if he had seen his son-in-law in prospect fucking his beloved daughter Eliza into fits, or administering a hot clyster of spunk up her arse-hole, he would have looked at the scene with delightful eyes, and given the performers his fatherly benediction.

'Well sir,' remarked Mrs Goater, 'if you like to sleep here tonight, as no doubt you will choose to do, you shall be made very comfortable – and you can pick out any one or two of the young ladies here as your bedfellow. They will show you some delicious little performances between themselves that will make your prick stand whether you like it or not, and when it does so, they will treat you with such voluptuous lubricity as you would never have experienced if you had been married a hundred years.'

This matronly advice being warmly seconded by Captain Torrant, who added a recommendation to the effect that one of the girls should be French, and Mrs Goater having recommended an experienced demoiselle called Juliette, and one named Maria, as her companion, the delighted Bonham was shown into a most luxurious chamber, feeling more like a he-goat or a young bull than a sanctimonious elder of the chapel which he patronized.

We have quite enough to do to follow his fortunes, so shall not at present trouble ourselves about Messrs. Archer and Torrant. Indeed we may safely leave those inexperienced gentlemen to take care of themselves.

In the morning, however, Mr Bonham was exhausted and no mistake. Never since his honeymoon had he felt so thoroughly fucked out, and not even then, for the late Mrs Bonham was a model of propriety; strong in her own person, strenuously resisted such lover-like, not to say sensual proceedings, as fucking upon the sofa, easy chair, up against the wall, in an arbour in the garden, and so forth; so it was rarely that the bridegroom was able to satisfy his longings, except in the legitimate place, namely, bed, and then, in the dark. So that when his handsome companions had retired to make their toilettes, desiring him to ring for anything he required, he was agreeably surprised upon doing so to find the bell answered by his dutiful nephew, who was accompanied by a slavey bearing a large dish of opened oysters and two or three bottles and tumblers.

The experienced young soldier insisted on his uncle immediately swallowing a half a tumbler of brandy and soda-water which was exceedingly grateful to his heated palate. Then he urged upon him the advisability of devouring as many oysters as he could possibly stow away.

They would, he said, give tone to his stomach, strength to his nerves and fresh vigour to his physical capabilities.

'Ha, hum!' said the elderly gentleman, in an assenting tone, 'that I think will be rather needful. I have taken more than one maidenhead in my times, I have fucked your aunt of Blessed memory, for nearly a month at a time hand-running, but never, never have I experienced such a night as I have just passed. Those girls are perfect devils for fucking. Why, Alfred, my dear boy, if you will believe me, they fucked each other!'

'Oh, I know,' replied Alfred, 'that was Juliette's performance, I suppose.'

'Yes,' said his uncle, 'that tall, black-haired girl, when she saw I was temporarily used up, laid Maria down pulled her thighs open and got into her as if she herself had been a man. At first I thought that was all make-believe but seeing Maria beginning to wriggle her rump, I looked carefully at the process, and I'll be damned,' continued Mr Bonham, forgetting his sanctity in his surprise and lust, 'if her clitoris was not sticking out of the lips of her cunt – more than an inch-and-a-half and was working into Maria like a cock, a small one certainly, but effective. Well this excited me so greatly that I got new vigour, and taking advantage of Juliette's prostrate position, I made my first successful attempt at getting into a girl's bum-hole. Dear me,' said the worthy country gentleman, 'what a novice I have been, and what a number of delightful and comparatively innocent pleasures, I have in my ignorance debarred myself from. Much allowance must be made of course, for the novelty in my case, but I don't think I ever enjoyed myself so much in my whole life before; and what's more, the girl liked it too! or if she did not, she is a most accomplished actress, and it does her a good deal of credit. And my honest old cock has hardly had ten minutes peace all night; but I must say that these oysters and brandy have refreshed me extremely, and I am much obliged to you, Alfred, for your forethought.'

'Well sir,' replied the promising youth, meekly, 'you know where to come now. Of course you never intend to get married again at this time of day.' (Which was an artful speech of Master Alfred's and his uncle felt rather conscious.) 'And you are very fresh and vigorous, better than many a younger man, and it is a pity that you cannot enjoy yourself in a comfortable, bachelorlike, legitimate way. Why should you bury yourself and Eliza in that dismal hole at Rutsden? Excuse me sir but it is rather a dreary place, when you might have a pretty villa at Richmond or Twickenham, with a pretty mistress keeping house for you, and you, yourself at liberty to visit your club, take dinners at Greenwich, or pay a visit to our esteemed hostess, Mrs Goater, or to inspect her cabinet of choice curiosities by way of a change, whenever you felt disposed.'

That idea seemed to strike Mr Bonham very favourably. A new vista in his career was opening to him. He had a very strong notion to partake of a pretty linnet (at present at Mrs Moreen's) that would exactly suit such a cage as Alfred suggested at Richmond, or elsewhere.

As for marriage, or any such moral proceeding, that faded from before his eyes, his excuse to himself was that in a married man promiscuous fucking would be objectionable, and he foretold that he had not paid his last visit to Mrs Goater's by many a one.

By this time it was eleven o'clock, the Lieutenant had taken himself out of the way, thinking that very probably the uncle and nephew would have some business affairs to arrange which might turn to the advantage of his chosen friend and comrade Torrant. And indeed the affair seemed likely to turn out in this way. For the first thing Mr Bonham did was to call Mrs Goater and request her to summon the young girls who had given him such unqualified pleasure.

Among them he distributed all the loose cash he had about him, and it was no inconsiderable amount either, while Mrs Goater was remunerated by a handsome cheque on his London bankers, for which she professed herself, and no doubt sincerely felt, very much obliged.

As for the girls, their gratitude knew no bounds. They half smothered the two gentlemen with lascivious kisses, and treated them to sundry exhibitions of their shapes and private parts, which brought on sundry fingerings and feelings. These farewell proceedings the young ladies doubtless considered would preserve their charms in the memory of the gentlemen, and probably they were right enough.

On leaving the hospitable mansion, Alfred proposed adjourning to his hotel, where they could have an early lunch on broiled bones, stewed oysters and sundry restoratives of that nature. But his business like uncle affirmed that he must first of all visit his banker, both to replenish his exhausted purse and make other arrangements.

We may imagine that Alfred was by no means indifferent to taking a ride with his honoured relative in the direction of the Bank. He fancied that somehow or other, especially after the evening they had spent, something to his advantage was pretty certain to turn up. Nor was this idea of his without foundation; for Mr Bonham had been considering that to get rid of his daughter was absolutely necessary, before entering upon any of his newly hatched schemes of felicity. Therefore after the elderly gentleman had drawn the pretty heavy cheque on his own account, he agreeably surprised the young gentleman by asking what amount would be absolutely required for the Majority which would immediately become vacant upon the retirement of the piously disposed Major Pobjoy. Alfred specified the amount with a small margin, and to his delight it was immediately transferred to his credit by the orders of his generous uncle. Nor was this all, for when the uncle and nephew were parting that afternoon, the elder gentleman pressed into the hand of the younger a bank note of pleasant amount, accompanying the gift by saying:

'I think Alf, that it would be as well to consider my visit to London had been specially made to arrange this little business of yours. Such an account of my London excursion will shut Eliza's mouth, of course and she is devilish curious, and saucy too, when she thinks that I have been doing something that she does not approve of; for I daresay you know her as well as I do.'

'A deuced sight better, old boy,' thought Alfred to himself.

'And at any rate, you will agree with me that it won't do to tell tales out of school.'

'Certainly not, sir,' gravely replied the Captain, 'and both for your sake and my own, I will take care to represent this visit of yours to London as only on matters referring to your own business and partly on mine. I can easily show that it is so by your kindness to me. I presume sir,' he continued, 'that upon my obtaining my step, there will be no objection on your part to my urging Miss Bonham to fix an early date to our marriage?'

'As early as you like, my boy,' responded the other, whose heart was considerably warmed and enlarged by the rakish proceedings he had just been initiated into. 'As soon as the young lady can ascertain from her milliner what is the latest fucking fashion – I mean the newest fashionable carriage dress – and get together a new assortment of drawers, chemises, and silk stockings, though heaven knows she ought to have plenty. She has cost me enough for such things in the last few years, but of course she must have them entirely new. It is a part of the sacred rite of marriage, I suppose. And then there is a little money to be made over to her, but that won't take the lawyers very long, I should think. You ought to be pretty comfortable, Alfred,' concluded the old buck, as he shook hands with his nephew.

Alfred, after seeing him fairly off on his road home, went to his club, and before ordering his dinner, on the principle of 'business before pleasure,' we suppose, indited a note to his beloved Eliza, which contained among the usual expressions of fond affection, compliments to her charms delicate or indelicate (as may happen) allusions to the happy two days they had recently spent (the garden privy scene was referred to with so much enthusiasm that Eliza fairly blushed which was somewhat unusual for her) and so on to the following passage:

'I have not seen the young lady you recommended to my notice as yet; but shall make a point of doing so tomorrow if possible. Of course, with the remembrance of your delicious person and lovely private parts, before my eyes and enshrined in my heart, it is mere blasphemy for me to think of being fond of any other girl; and if I fuck your young acquaintance, Miss Fielding, it is entirely as a matter of business. Of course, I don't wish to do anything of the sort; but it seems to be necessary for our mutual happiness – and it is enough that my Eliza requests me to do so. I sacrifice myself to do her behests! Duty calls and I obey!'

What a fine soldierly feeling young Captain Torrant had, even where fucking was concerned.

But this letter, wherein he so nobly announced his determination to do his duty under all circumstances, was not the only bit of correspondence which he achieved before sitting down to his dinner. The next day Mrs Moreen received the following note.

Dear Madam:

Instead of leaving town as I expected to-day, I have yielded to the solicitations of my deceased wife's sister, Mrs Smith, to dine at her house. She particularly wishes to see my ward, Miss Fielding, and though my request may appear to be somewhat out of rule, perhaps you will indulge me so far as to let Rosa be dressed by four in the afternoon, when either myself, or my nephew, Captain Torrant, who is a steady and amiable young man, will call for the young lady to escort her to Mrs Smith's.

This letter with the usual polite formulary, was signed 'H Bonham' and after signing and addressing it, and transmitting it to the post, Captain Torrant was conscious of having performed his duty, at the cost of considerable exertion and self denial, and sat down to his dinner with healthy appetite. We can easily imagine the glee with which Rosa received Mrs Moreen's announcement that she was to dress herself to go out to dinner with her guardian, and of course her chosen friends and room-mates were not long unacquainted with the happiness in store for her. Charlotte affected to pooh-pooh, the whole affair, saying that Rosa had never been 'Brought out' and had no business to be going to a dinner party.

But Harriet Lovit sympathized with her pleasure, and impressed upon her mind that she was to bring back an exact account of the ladies' dresses, and especially of the appearance of the gentlemen.

'I wonder dear,' she said, 'if your guardian's nephew, Captain what's-his-name, will call for you instead of the old gentleman! That would be fine! If he does – and from what you say it seems likely enough – mind you don't let him feel your cunt, or fuck you in the carriage. It will rumple your dress and make your hair untidy!'

'My goodness Harriet, you cannot imagine a young

gentleman being alone with a young lady ten minutes without feeling her or fucking her, or something else of the kind.'

'Well my dear, I only speak from my own experience, and I should not wonder, if, after taking a short drive with a young officer, you will not be able to talk about your experience also.'

In due time a neat brougham brought not Mr Bonham, but Captain Torrant, who behaved himself most demurely towards Mrs Moreen. Not that his affectation of a staid and precise demeanour was at all necessary, for after receiving Mr Bonham's note, she would have entrusted one of her pupils to old Nick himself, and washed her hands of the consequences.

'It is rather a long way to Great Poke-hole Place,' remarked Captain Torrant to his lovely companion, when they had started on their ride. 'Would you like to have the blinds down – the glare of the sun is rather strong?'

With this, without waiting for Rosa's consent, he suited the action to the word. Rosa might have objected, wishing not only to see but be seen, but then the young dragoon was a particularly handsome young fellow, and there was something fascinating in the fact of taking a long drive with him, quite in private as it were.

'I understand, beautiful Miss Fielding,' began Alfred in a tone of respectful admiration, 'that there is some chance of you becoming my aunt. I am sure I admire my uncle Bonham's good taste; and I shall be very proud of having such a lovely young aunt, and I hope you will be very cruel and severe to his daughter Eliza and me.'

'Oh, sir, how can you talk in such a way?' replied the blushing Rosa, 'I am sure I shall hardly know how to conduct myself properly as Mrs Bonham, and as an aunt to such a – a – young gentleman as you are.'

'Never mind, Miss Fielding, I am going to marry Miss

Bonham,' was the encouraging reply, 'and I'll ask her to love you for my sake, she can refuse me nothing.'

'Ah, I don't wonder at that,' replied Rosa, quite off her guard.

'Don't you indeed?' said the gentleman, 'then perhaps you will grant me a kiss upon the strength of our approaching relationship.'

Rosa smiled, and turned up her sweet face and ripe lips towards her nephew-that-was-to-be, who immediately took advantage of the opportunity. She kissed him once and in return he kissed her about half a dozen times, and then began to roll his tongue into her mouth. This second performance surprised Rosa not a little, for it had never been part of Mr Bonham's proceedings. Still, she felt the indescribable excitement and voluptuous titillation which the operation inevitably induced, and never thought of preventing him from doing as he liked, until he, and perhaps she too, began to think of some further proceedings. Captain Torrant knelt by her side and holding one of her hands while with the other he was gently and cautiously feeling her ankles:

'What a happy man my uncle must be!' he remarked, 'he has told me how deliciously pure and beautiful you are in your concealed limbs and those delicate parts, which no mortal eye has ever beheld, except his, I suppose.'

And here the young gentleman paused, astutely wishing to entrap Rosa into some acknowledgement as to whether his esteemed uncle had managed to get into her or not. She certainly felt rather confused and blushed a good deal, but managed to carry the matter off pretty well by saying;

'Pray sir, if it is usual for gentlemen when they are about to marry ladies to know as much about them as you would seem to imply; perhaps, as you seem to know so much about it, Miss Bonham has permitted you the extraordinary favour of peeping into her charms? I should think they must be something most magnificent.'

'Ah, my beautiful relative!' exclaimed the lively Captain, 'you thought you could catch me, did you? No, no, one secret for another if you please! If you'll betray my uncle's secrets, I'll betray his daughter's – that is only fair.'

'But,' said Rosa, laughing, 'in betraying Mr Bonham's secrets I should betray my own, and it is hardly fair to make me do that, is it?'

'No, it is not,' replied Alfred, in a high state of excitement, 'and so I shall find it out for myself. Now sweet Rosa, it is of no use for you to struggle or resist, I mean to have a peep and a feel, so be kind enough to put your pretty little feet upon the opposite seat. There now,' (as she did so) 'that will be snug and comfortable. Bless us, what darling little white kid boots and silk stockings! The old governor has more taste in young ladies' dress than I gave him credit for. And now for the inspection of your young thighs and precious little cunt.'

'Oh, no, Captain Torrant, you must not,' exclaimed Rosa, 'indeed I could not allow it!'

At the same time she was gradually stretching her thighs open while the handsome young fellow felt and opened the lips of her all but virgin cunt, whose aspect, however, evidently betrayed that the invader and destroyer had been there.

'You have been fucked,' exclaimed the delighted Alfred, 'a slice from a cut loaf can never be missed, and as it is all in the family, as the saying goes, I shall–'

Here he interrupted himself by shoving his tongue into the lady's sore and somewhat inflamed parts, while he unfastened his braces and unbuttoned his trousers.

'Oh dear Captain Torrant, how indelicate! and the carriage will be stopping directly, I know it will, and you will rumple my silk dress so.'

We hope our readers admire the force of the young lady's objections to being fucked in a carriage. The gallant dragoon set them at naught, requesting her to take up her dresses — as completely and as carefully as she could — he would take care of her petticoats and chemise; as for the carriage stopping, he affirmed that it was a long way from Clapham to Great Poke-hole Place, and they would not arrive there for half-an-hour.

'So, now dearest Rosa,' he continued directing his charger towards the gap in her pretty hedge.

'But you have not kept faith with me,' she cried in a pretty affectation of pretending not to know what he was doing. 'You have not told me whether you ever got into your beautiful cousin's private parts — Oh!'

The last exclamation was produced by the effectual insertion of the gentleman's cock; the milk and water, recommended by Mr Bonham had been effectual but not altogether so — hence the slight involuntary scream. But now her companion was well in and quite comfortable, as kneeling upon one of the carriage cushions, he was ramming into the young girl, immensely to his own satisfaction, while he stimulated her lusts and reconciled her to the proceedings, by repeating in broken sentences and somewhat exaggerated terms, some of his adventures with Miss Bonham, interspersed with the episodes of Bob fucking and buggering Lucy in the stables, and Major Ringtail fucking Miss Larcher in the chapel, to the great satisfaction and edification of the minister of the word, as Stiggins called himself, and to such of the congregation as were fortunate enough to catch a glimpse of the lady's legs over the side of the pew. This last apocryphal adventure, Captain Torrant related as an actual fact, thinking that as Rosa probably knew the principal actress in the scene, she would not only be interested and instructed, but consider her present predicament an innocent one in comparison.

104

And he was quite right, Rosa richly enjoyed the description of her future step-daughter's black haired cunt and long white legs and snowy rump. She began to wriggle her bottom with delight at the vivid description given by Alfred of his man's laudable endeavours to split up Lucy's arse hole, and when it came to the chapel scene, she murmured:

'Miss Susan Larcher! – so respectable – in chapel! Her legs over the pew – and one of the officers right into her in broad daylight! – and her revered pastor watching the performance! – Oh! – oh – h – h Captain Torrant.'

This was the crisis of the performance, and silence reigned in the carriage, unbroken except by a still, small sound, as of kissing. Then, after a few minutes calm, Captain Torrant arose, and buttoning his trousers told Rosa there would never be any reason for making the most distant allusion to anyone as to what had taken place, or what their conversation had been about which, as may be imagined, Rosa promised for her own sake, readily enough. Then drawing up the blinds, as Rosa pulled down her clothes, her Majesty's officer put his head out of the window and told Thomas he might drive as fast as he liked – now. A very significant proof that his proceedings had been premeditated. Then turning to his lovely companion, he told her not to be startled by anything she saw at Mrs Smith's house, and particularly not to be frightened if she did not find her guardian there. At this Rosa stared at first, but by degrees a light seemed to break in upon her, and she exclaimed laughing:

'Oh! I see now! How wicked of you Captain Torrant, deceiving my venerable school-mistress, taking advantage of my unprotected innocence, and forging your uncle's name! Don't you know what a crime forgery is, sir? – and that you deserve to be hung?'

'Hung around your neck, if you like, you sweet, saucy witch!' exclaimed the Captain, clasping the young beauty in his arms, and imprinting a dozen luscious kisses on her lips.

In fact his proceedings were becoming so very forcible that Rosa was obliged to tell him the blinds were up, and that they must be getting near their destination, if it was in London at all: and finally that she did not want her hair and her mauve silk dress more tumbled than it was. Captain Torrant assured her that this was a matter of no consequence, and that it would not be noticed; that even if it were, the good natured ladies and gentlemen to whom he would introduce her would take it all as a matter of course, and promised that she would have an elegant dinner and a merry evening.

To these allurements Rosa made no sort of objection, merely striking a bargain with Captain Torrant that she should be sent back to Mrs Moreen's in good time, for as the girl very sensibly observed, a night's pleasure was all very well. She was duly sensible of Captain Torrant's admiration, and the loving affection he had shown to her, but still it would never do to run the risk of losing Mr Bonham's favour and protection, which would be inevitably the case, if she were reported absent from the Academy all night.

Now with a different kind of girl, Captain Torrant would have felt disposed to treat an interloper between him and his uncle's favour by fucking her as hard as he could, and allowing any of his dissipated companions, who they were about to meet, to do what they liked with her. A little sodomy might be the prescription suitable to the development of her faculties and rump-hole – and then having given her as much wine (and a trifle more) than was good for her – leave her to find her way to Clapham as best she could or go to the devil, if this proceeding suited her better. But Rosa was such a sweet pretty girl, and she surrendered her delicious young charms to him with such a tender grace, that the Captain, moved by emotions of gratitude for the luscious fuck he had just enjoyed, and with a lively sense of expectation of fucks to come, not only during the present evening, but when Miss Fielding became his uncle's mistress, vowed and declared with all sincerity, that she should be delivered safe and sound at Clapham Academy.

He reflected that the money for his Majority was deposited; that his cousin's hand was promised to him; and he knew his uncle better than to suppose he would not give his daughter a handsome dowry, which with the money she had inherited from her mother, and his pay and private means, would make them very well off indeed.

'And I am sure,' mused Torrant to himself, 'that after the conversation I had the other morning with the old boy, he will not think of getting married at all, and Rosa, and two or three natural children of his or my begetting, will not stand in the way of Eliza's succession: so I will not ruin the dear little chit. I will only fuck her dreadfully and send her back to Mrs Moreen's with a sore cunt, to set her two or three bedroom confidantes longing for prick, by the interesting adventures she will have to relate to them.'

Having come to this virtuous resolution, the young officer relaxed his thoughtful features, calling a playful remonstrance from Rosa as to what he could possibly be thinking of, with so grave a face, and whether he considered it polite to leave a young lady, whom he had been professing so much regard for, all by herself? This produced a playful and affectionate rejoinder, and indeed Rosa was in danger of displaying to the eyes of the outer world the colour of her elastic garters, and other little private matters in those directions, when the carriage drew up at the door of an oldish looking house, but evidently well built and in a state of high preservation.

'This, my sweet little pet,' observed her conductor, 'is

one of the houses of the Earl of Longbowles. I think,' he added, laughing, 'that your dear friend, Mrs Moreen, will be rather puzzled to discover the address of Mr Bonham's widowed sister by turning up the list of 'Smiths' in either the Court or Trade directory. And if you are cross questioned on the subject, my beauty, you can mention any jumble of street names that occur to you first (you have such a bad head for streets, you know) and you can mention having met Mrs Smith, and your guardian, and the Earl of Longbowles. Allow me to assist you to alight.'

So saying, with great courtesy, he handed Rosa out of the carriage, saying to the coachman as he did so:

'Half past eleven, sharp – mind Thomas!'

So it certainly looked as if he meant to keep his promise to Rosa.

As our friends were uncloaking in the hall, the Earl of Longbowles emerged from his study, which was on the ground floor. He was a fine looking middle-aged man with a bearing about him that showed in some degree the marks of the fast life he had led from an early age. He greeted Torrant cordially, exclaiming:

'Ah, Alfred my boy, how are you? Very glad to see you and your fair friend. And what a pretty girl!' continued he, surveying Rosa with the air of a connoisseur. 'Is she as good as she looks, Alf?' he asked, with an expression that brought the colour into Rosa's face.

'I assure your Lordship that she is a sweet creature in every respect,' was Torrant's reply, as he pressed Rosa's arm to reassure her.

'Well,' said the Earl, 'you had better go upstairs to the drawing room. You will find a select party of our friends there – fine men and fair women! I will follow you directly.'

And his Lordship was as good as his word, indeed a

good deal better, for instead of following them after the delay of a minute or two, as any one might have supposed from his speech, he followed them instantly, being rather curious to have a more intimate inspection of Rosa. Accordingly, when the young lady was half upstairs, leaning on her protector's arm, she was not a little startled by feeling her clothes gently, but effectually raised from behind, and a hot kiss pressed upon one of the cheeks of her bum. At the same time a half smothered voice remarked:

'Delicious indeed! Very fine legs, too!' And then his Lordship, emerging from her graceful drapery, remarked in a business way: 'She'll do, Alfred, she'll do very well! She is fit to show up with the finest in the room!'

Rosa was indignant, and disposed to be very angry, but Torrant whispered to her not to mind it, that one must do at Rome as Rome does, and that his Lordship submitted to a similar inspection almost every lady that entered his house – at any rate, this particular house.

His Lordship, he also informed her, had some peculiar tastes and lusts; and she should see some curious scenes, but he told her not to be frightened, but to eat a good dinner, and to enjoy herself as much as she possibly could.

And Rosa, who now felt she was 'in for it', as the saying is, wisely determined to follow his advice and make the best of her situation.

Chapter VI

Rosa was of course a little fluttered by the exciting nature of the incident produced by her noble host's behaviour on the staircase, but she still possessed enough presence of mind to walk into the drawing room of the Earl's mansion, hanging on Captain Torrant's arm, with as good a grace, and as cool an aspect, (or nearly so) as if nothing particular had taken place during her transit between the hall door and the top of the staircase. In the drawing room, she was both astonished and delighted, delighted by the brilliant appearance of the room, and astonished at the magnificent display of beautiful women and handsome men; such as the Earl of Longbowles usually invited to join his circle. Indeed his Lordship, who could afford to suit his own fancies, invariably declared that he liked to have good looking people about him – small blame to him for that! and displayed his taste, not only with regard to his judgement in hiring chambermaids and waiting maids, but also in respect to the young gentlemen and ladies he invited to his entertainments. And on this occasion, Rosa was quite bewitched by the galaxy of beauty exhibited by the women she saw; some of them kept-mistresses; some of them young demoiselles from a fashionable house of a certain repute, and some neglected wives, who in the unpleasant predicament of having married old men for the sake of money and a fine establishment, had found out later in the day, that jewellery and coaches and horses, were not the only luxuries that a young bride required, and were glad to make their appearance at Lord Longbowles' evening parties, to obtain what every young lady – aye and a good many elderly ladies too – consider the indispensable requisite: prick! and a downright good fucking.

And to show how cleverly his Lordship had forseen the wants of his guests in this particular, there were certain curtained recesses established, furnished with well cushioned ottomans; wherein gentlemen and ladies, who felt all excited by their delightful proximity in the waltz, or their companionship during the luxurious supper, might relieve the inevitable tendency, which such luxurious proceedings might create in their minds and bodies.

Our readers can understand that Captain Torrant was not very long in making Rosa understand the meaning of these little accommodation recesses, nor did she, on her part, blush more than a charming girl should do, at being made to understand the purpose for which they were intended, and being shown the deliciously licentious pictures that decorated their walls. But she did colour up prettily, when the Earl of Longbowles, who had by this time entered the apartment, begged to be introduced to Captain Torrant's pretty partner, (just as if he had never seen her before) and after making some outrageously complimentary remarks about her beautiful face said:

'I say Alfred, you have such very good taste in girl's shapes and general capabilities, that I have no doubt that Miss Fielding's hidden charms are quite equal to those she openly displays. Permit me the luxury of kissing her thighs and bottom, – you have a right to her other choice

111

delicacies.'

To this announcement, Rosa was going to offer a feeble protest, saying something about so many ladies and gentlemen being present; but instead of the ladies being shocked, a good many of the couples present, who no doubt were pretty well initiated into his Lordship's proceedings, came up and declared, that as a young stranger, she must, of course, 'pay her footing', and that they would like nothing better than to see the charms of a young novice exposed, as they certainly would be during his Lordship's intended proceedings.

Captain Torrant, moreover, began to loosen his trouser's front, as if he on his part did not intend to be an idle spectator of the bottom-kissing operation; nor, to tell the truth, did Rosa wish that he should be. She had been a good deal excited by witnessing sundry performances among the well-paired couples present, and felt proportionately kindly disposed; much more apparently than did the beautiful Mrs Courville, who, wedded to an old and worn out husband, had up to this time amused herself with encouraging young men, almost but not quite to the point of opening her thighs. But a lady who encourages young men up to a certain point finds out sooner or later that her passions may betray her, and on this occasion the virtuous Mrs Courville betrayed herself. She was leaning on the arm of Mr Harcourt, who had long been a suitor for her favours, and who had probably had more wet dreams and frigged himself oftener in the nightly contemplations of her charms than anyone else of her thousand admirers. And so it came to pass, that when she saw Captain Torrant deliberately raise up Rosa's dress in front, while Lord Longbowles did the young lady the same kind of office behind, her feelings so long restrained, broke forth with a vengeance. And no wonder, for Rosa's exhibition was splendid. She was dressed for a ball, and as graceful and delicate as a young lady of taste is, as a matter of course, upon such an occasion. Consequently when, under the impulse of the behind and front pressure, she began to open her thighs, she provoked the admiration of all the company present.

Lord Longbowles, as we may easily imagine, was not satisfied with kissing her rump, but as Alfred Torrant got into her cunt, he performed the same kind office for her bum-hole; a part which his Lordship had a peculiar fancy for, and for which he had capability; his cock being one of the long and slender description and rather more easily inserted.

In Rosa's case this was rather fortunate as she was enabled to enjoy her lover's operation without feeling any irksome affects from doing double duty. Of the effects produced we may judge from Mrs Courville's remarks, who exclaimed to the enraptured young man who held her on his arm:

'Oh, Arthur, only look at that sweet girl's thighs! – and see how Captain Torrant is ramming it into her! How she does seem to enjoy it! I wonder if she appreciates his Lordship's performance at any rate as much as he does? There's no mistake about that! Just look at him driving into her! There – he has done now!'

Those interesting observations were made as the crisis was taking place, and all three of the actors arrived at the desired goal and spunked together. Naturally Rosa contributed to give Captain Torrant his share of the delight which he had been giving her, but it is doubtful if even under that delightful reciprocity, whether the handsome dragoon experienced more pleasure than did his partner, the Earl.

Every man to his taste, say we, and on this occasion, if his Lordship did not gratify his taste, it's a pity!

He had inspected Rosa's beautiful legs and milk-white rump during her ascent of the stairs, he had acquired by so doing a tremendous prick-stand; and he had been able to quench that raging fire in the bowels of the loveliest and sweetest girl in the world; and if he was not pleased, he ought to have been – that's all!

Now the effect upon the Earl we shall describe presently; in the meantime we have to refer to the case of Mrs Courville.

'What are you doing, Arthur?' was the first thing she said. 'You should not do that, you know!'

But this we must inform our readers was very feebly and hesitatingly said after all.

'Good heavens, Arthur,' she continued, 'what a colour has got into your cheeks, what a fire in your eyes! Ah, you are doing wrong to a married woman, you know you are, and I shouldn't allow you, but – but – somehow I can't stop it. Oh, pray, pray don't hurt me!'

The reader can readily understand from our illustration that this broken form of words (we can hardly call it conversation) was being carried on while Mr Harcourt was lifting up her silk robes and underclothing and inspecting and feeling too – what he had for so many years longed for. And who can blame him! He had been thinking of Blanche Courville's legs, her cunt, her bottom, all her charms, in fact for many and many a long day; and now when he caught the lady, a little excited and disposed to be compliant, would he not be a dreadful idiot not to take advantage of the delicious feast offered him?

Well he did, and the company present, some of whom, the gentlemen at least, had thought Mrs Courville unapproachable were surprised and delighted by seeing her well clad legs, alternately lifted into the air and laid over a gentleman's back, as she exclaimed:

'Arthur dear, do please recollect, that it is almost a maidenhead that you are taking! – do pray be merciful!'

But Mr Harcourt had been hungry for his feast for a long time and had no mercy; and indeed we hold with the

114

doctors, that in cases where the patient requires operation, quick performance is best. Whether or no on this
occasion the beautiful and virtuous Mrs Courville,
found out what was meant by a fine, handsome man's
prick stuck up her, somewhere near her kidneys, as she
fancied, the said gentleman's finger being rammed up
her arsehole, with the idea apparently of finding out how
her digestion was.

The appreciation of his Lordship and his guests was
something wonderful to witness.

Both the young gentlemen and young ladies seemed to
unite in their approbation of Mrs Courville's pride being
taken down. They said they did not understand what
pride meant, by encouraging young fellows to band
about her, and again to come to the notorious Earl of
Longbowles' evening parties.

But Rosa was more gentle-hearted. As Mr Harcourt
withdrew his prick out of its beautiful sheath, and began
to button himself up, leaving his charming friend partially exhausted on the couch, Rosa came to her, remarking:

'If you would excuse the liberty from an entire
stranger, Mrs Courville, and permit me to wipe you, I
shall be very happy I assure you.'

So saying, and without waiting for assent, she produced her lawn pocket handkerchief, and proceeded to
wipe the besmeared cunt of Mrs Courville, who could
only remark in reply:

'You sweet, kind, girl, I can only wish you the same
pleasure that I have experienced!'

'Tell me, Torrant, candidly if you will, whether you
are sincerely attached to your pretty companion?' asked
his Lordship, addressing the Captain, on the first opportunity he had of speaking to him privately.

'Well, my Lord,' replied the gallant officer, 'You can
see for yourself that she is very nice and fresh; indeed I

consider that she has hardly been fucked at all; for although when I got into her – for the first time – I found she had no maidenhead, that may easily have occurred by some other means than a man's prick, for she is at present at a fashionable ladies' finishing school, and I need not tell a gentleman of your Lordship's experience that what with candles, dildoes, and each other's fingers, the young ladies become as open as if they had been married for twenty months.'

'Bless her sweet face and lovely bottom,' exclaimed the peer, 'I should like to buy her from you, Captain Torrant.'

'Oh, dear me, pray don't talk that way, my Lord,' responded Alfred politely, 'I have a certain regard for her of course; but I want to keep her out of my uncle's way (your Lordship knows the rich Mr Bonham of Rutsden Lodge?) and my own cousin Eliza told me she was afraid of his marrying her, which of course would play the devil with my expectations, and Eliza's too; so I thought that if Rosa got a jolly good fucking, it would be pleasant for her and deprive her of the chance of becoming my aunt; though by the way, I should not wonder if the old boy made her his mistress. That would not be so bad; but even then she might have a family! and I would very much rather see her in the position of your mistress than presiding over Rutsden Lodge in any capacity. Miss Bonham requested me to roger her, but if I should carry out the practice to any great extent, that young lady might be addicted to jealousy, so that if your Lordship would take her off my hands and uncle's, and make the dear little thing a good allowance, everybody will be pleased.'

'Well,' replied his Lordship in a reflecting tone, 'I have only one objection to make, she is rather young, and I decidedly require someone with a little experience. You know, Alfred, my boy, that when a man gets to my time of life, he needs certain little refinements in his lasciviousness, such as only a well-trained woman can supply.'

'I understand,' responded the younger gentleman knowingly. 'A little preparatory frigging, or some provocative sucking, an opportune exhibition of plump white posteriors, such as your Lordship seemed to appreciate just now, and no hesitation in submitting the luxurious orifice appertaining thereto to your worship's penetrating prick, while occasionally perhaps a little judicious birching.'

'Ah, I see you understand all about it!' replied the Earl, laughingly interrupting his guest, 'I only wish there was no necessity for my resorting to such stimulants. However, it is a great comfort when one knows where to get them, and if you have no objection, I will consult your little friend as to her capacity and willingness.'

'No objection in life,' returned Alfred, 'I did promise to take her back to Clapham tonight, but if your Lordship makes a satisfactory arrangement with her, she will be quite independent of Mrs Moreen, or my uncle either. Let us withdraw into this alcove and talk to her.'

'Certainly,' said the peer, 'and I'll give her half a pint of champagne with a spoonful of brandy in it, and if that doesn't excite her and make her half tipsy, the devil is in it, and there is always a dildo kept in one of the cupboards.'

Rosa approached Captain Torrant at this moment saying with a half coquettish air:

'Well sir, I think it is time for me to be getting back to Clapham, you seem so much engaged that I suppose that my company has no longer any attractions for you. I am sure I am very much obliged to you for the attentions you have paid to my humble person, and hope that his Lordship has been gratified, but I suppose that you are no

117

better than the rest of your sex, and having enjoyed my poor little body, such as it is, you don't want me any longer.'

'Indeed Miss Fielding,' replied his Lordship, politely, 'you do discredit to your own attractions, and barely justice to the sensibilities of Captain Torrant and myself. I was just expressing myself in very warmest terms as to yourself and your charms and was consulting my friend here, as to whether you would be willing to leave his uncle's protection for mine; and I must do him justice and say that on his part he seems very unwilling to let you go.'

'Oh, but he must, sooner or later,' remarked Rosa, very briskly, 'I am very glad to contribute to his pleasure, and he fucks me very charmingly and tenderly, and I am sure I try to meet him half way don't I Alfred?' continued the laughing girl, 'but his cock is devoted henceforth to a more legitimate business, and Miss Bonham would half murder me if she knew how often and what lengths he has pierced into my person. She has a black-haired cunt, hasn't she, Alfred? And I shouldn't wonder if she had a dark fringe around her bottom hole.'

'God bless me!' exclaimed the delighted Earl, 'how knowing we are! How on earth can such a young and inexperienced girl as you are, have picked up such information?'

'From my schoolfellow, Harriet Lovit,' was Rosa's reply. 'She is something like Miss Bonham, though rather younger, and she has black hair and plenty of it. She is a very hot-blooded and lustful girl, and I have seen her exhibit herself, back and front fifty times. Indeed she is very fond of sucking my cunt, and running my finger into her bottom-hole.'

'And I dare say Miss Rosa, if you were to tell the truth she has sucked you many and many a time,' retorted the Earl. 'I suppose young ladies at boarding schools regard spunk good for their complexions? At any rate they seem to get a good deal of it over their cheeks and noses. I wonder how yours would set upon my moustache, it is growing rather grey and wants some reviving fluid.'

At this speech Captain Torrant began to laugh, and Rosa was beginning to give expression to a blushing denial, but a tumbler of champagne – slyly laced with brandy – conquered her scruples; and she consented to accommodate herself to the Earl's fanciful lusts. This was performed by her perching herself astride his face, as indeed, she was not unaccustomed to do, having put herself in the same position for a somewhat similar purpose with Miss Lovit. In this case however she had rather more duty to perform. His Lordship was by no means an exhausted man and still had plenty of semen in his physical nature, but with every desire to enjoy a perpetual cock-stand, he was deficient in that qualification except under unusual provocation.

Thus his walls were covered with licentious pictures, representing fucking, frigging and buggering under every aspect. His cupboards contained dozens of exciting books, and he had plenty of dildoes and birch-rods for the use of his handsome servant girls and beautiful lady visitors. On the present occasion when Rosa put her face down upon his private parts, she found his balls were round and firm, but that his prick was limp, but by no means despicably sized. However before inserting his tongue between her young, delicate, fair-haired cunt lips, he requested her to take his prick into her mouth. This the good natured girl did at once, laughing at the same time at having to perform the operation under the inspection of Captain Torrant.

As for the gallant officer, there was no mistake about his prick-stand, his breeches were so near splitting, that in order to save the stitches he had to open them and take out Master Priapus. But the worst of it was that he hardly knew what to do with it after he had got him out. There he was, cream-coloured shaft and ruby head, all ready and erect as you please, and no hole to shove him into. Rosa's mouth and tongue were occupied, she had got the Earl's tool to a beautiful state of stiffness, and was in a fair way of getting a tolerable mouthful of spunk. Her cunt was, as we have said, occupied by his Lordship's mouth and tongue, and his nose all but filled up her little bum hole. Besides as the reader can readily understand from the relative positions of the lascivious pair, it would have been next to impossible for Torrant to have poked that delicate orifice without stifling the noble Earl. After kissing and slapping Rosa's buttocks which were gently undulating with incipient pleasure, and shoving one of his fingers up the vacant hole, he was going to resort with a sigh to the poor expedient of frigging himself, when his noble host who was neither unobservant or selfish, gave his tongue a moment's holiday, and put it to its more legitimate use, by exclaiming, 'Don't do that, Torrant, I am afraid that all the gayer portion of my fair guests have provided themselves with partners, either in the dance or on the sofa, but there are still half a dozen pretty girls in the servant's hall and kitchen, or there is Lady Forepart. She is sure not to be engaged. To be sure she is five and thirty, and has taken an oath or solemn vow, or something of that kind, not to marry again, but she is a jolly widow enough, and if she is never to be married again that's no reason why she shouldn't be fucked, and I would recommend you to do it, whether she likes it or not. She is in mourning now for quite six months, and if she doesn't want some prick, she should do so – that's all. I shouldn't wonder if she kicks and struggles a good deal, but you don't mind that I suppose!'

'Certainly not,' replied the dragoon, 'I shall rather like it indeed, by way of a change. There is something piquant in rogering a virtuous woman against her will.'

'All right, bricky!' assented the Earl, resuming his occupation of stuffing his tongue up Rosa's cunt and licking her clitoris, for this perseverance was happily rewarded by receiving a small douche of that young lady's liquor all over his moustache and mouth, while Rosa was all but choked by the ejaculation which she simultaneously forced him to make.

When Alfred re-entered the room, he looked around in vain for Lady Forepart. But as women are always amiable to get each other into mischief, or to assist one another in the perpetration of any propriety, the prudent Mrs Harcourt (who did not want any more fucking just at present) and could so afford to be generous, on learning the object of Alfred's search, informed him that the widow had gone into the ladies retiring room to arrange her hair.

'And it is my opinion,' observed the knowing lady, 'that that may possibly mean something else, on the pot-de-chambre likely enough – for she ate a good deal of supper, and prudes must perform the necessities of nature in the way of evacuation just as well as anybody else. The pot is at the far side of the bed, and if you go in quietly and creep underneath, you may very probably find the precise Lady Forepart in the act of doing her little business, and have a good laugh at her mortification.'

Thanking Mrs Harcourt for her information, and chuckling to himself with the glee of a mischievous school boy, Captain Torrant proceeded to a large room especially provided for the accommodation of lady guests alone. Indeed from the nature of the orgies at his Lordship's mansion some place of easy access was absolutely necessary, for the retirement of the female guests; and though Lady Forepart had not been treated in such a way as to make it needful for her to make an instant rush to a chamber utensil, still she was availing herself of the accommodations afforded, and was moreover so busily engaged that she did not hear Alfred's entrance, or perceive his soft tread on the carpet. We hope our readers will not accuse us of indelicacy, when we say that he kept himself breathlessly silent, until the splendid woman rose and stooping from him, proceeded to use some soft paper in the necessary way.

Then the prospect of her great white arse, and its fully exposed orifice, slightly open from its recent duty; her round, plump thighs and her well turned muscular legs, made such an attractive ensemble, that although the lady was clad in the sombre garments of woe our young soldier found her irresistible. Perhaps the very fact of her unblemished character, her habiliments offering such a marked contrast to the gaily dressed company, together with her vow of chastity, all combined to render the fucking or ravishing such a lady a most desirable act.

At any rate he did no longer hesitate, but striding across the room, almost before the lady had time to finish her operation, he clasped her firmly round the belly with his left arm, while with his right hand he guided his prick to the lips of her somewhat capacious cunt, and lunged into her so furiously as to nearly set her on her head. She screamed out lustily for help, and 'mercy' declaring that 'a brutal lustful man was ramming her to death' and that she would fall on her face.

To all of which Captain Torrant replied by muttered praises of her splendid rump, vowing that he would get into her arse-hole before he had done with her, asking her why she did not lean against the wall or the bed for support. He had even the audacity to ask her whether she liked his cock, or that of her dear departed husband best! and when the insulted and outraged lady raised one of her handsome legs, and endeavoured by shoving it backwards to push him out of her person, he caught hold not only of that but the other leg as well and holding them both up, declared that he was 'particularly fond of a flying fuck' and that although her ladyship was rather heavy for such amusement, yet he would not mind a little exertion for her sake.

Then indeed, without waiting for or requiring an answer from the speechlessly indignant lady, he coaxed up his own lust by enquiring in a mock respectful tone, if she had ever been fucked before marriage, or if Lord Forepart had been lucky enough to have taken her virginity; whether the blood had trickled down her thighs; then cramming one of his fingers up her bum-hole, he kindly asked was that orifice in a state of virginity. And whether she thought it would bleed upon his driving his prick into it!

All these genteel remarks and questions the outraged Lady Forepart let pass in wrathful silence, but when his stalwart weapon began to produce its naturally expected result upon a fine young widow of six months, and she began to push out her rump to meet his shoves, and to wriggle in as lascivious a way as the most licentious woman in the saloon could do, she could no longer restrain her tongue.

'Don't flatter yourself, you brute that I am exhibiting these natural emotions from any affection for you! Any vigorous woman, deprived as I have latterly been, must do what I am doing now; and it would be all the same if a goat or a donkey or any other suitable sized animal got into my person.'

'All right, my lady,' was the cool reply, 'please yourself. Pray did his Lordship approve of such little games? Now that I come to inspect you more closely, you are tolerably well stretched; pray don't move yet, and I'll see what I can do toward knocking your two holes into one!'

With these words the lustful young soldier made use of some of the mingled juices which were liberally shed in his victim's orifice, to lubricate her lesser hole; the lady protesting that she knew he was going to marry his cousin Miss Bonham, and she would inform that young lady what a lustful tyrant she was about to unite her fate with.

Captain Torrant coolly remarked to that – that Eliza was perfectly acquainted with that peculiarity, and did not wish to have him otherwise, that he had rogered her well both back and front and believed that he had got her with child, that he was going to marry her in a fortnight, and would be very glad to see Lady Forepart at the wedding.

Finally drawing his prick out of her, before the exhausted lady could remonstrate, with a very creditable, and indeed unusual effort of lustful strength, he invaded (apparently her maiden) rectum. This produced a single scream, followed by a storm of sobs, tears, reproaches, from the now thoroughly finished widow; when, after receiving a half a dozen hard slaps on her outraged buttocks, she spent copiously, despite herself. Then she upped and ordered her carriage and took herself off, without saying good night to her host or any of his guests.

Rosa did not go home to Mrs Moreen that night, nor indeed any more. Like a wise girl, she considered that 'a bird in hand was worth two in the bush' and that the offer of a handsome income from his Lordship was worth more than the prospect – rather an uncertain one – of becoming Mrs Bonham.

That gentleman however behaved like a trump, (so Mrs Moreen considered at any rate) and consoled himself with keeping a neat little villa at Twickenham, and pretty frequent visits to Mrs Goater's establishment. That amiable lady still flourishes, and keeps around her the same delightful family of young ladies – or some very like them.

Captain Torrant was happily married to his cousin Eliza, and was almost as faithful a husband as could be reasonably expected from one of his natural character, and exposure to such temptations as were to be found in the attractions of the Earl of Longbowles' establishment and Mrs Goater's.

And now as we have accounted for the fate of the principal characters in our short story, we will bid our indulgent readers a cordial farewell.